RAYON THE DUST BUNNY

AND A VACUUM ABHORRED

An appliance fiction novel

A. Michael Collins

Copyright © 2016 A. Michael Collins

All rights reserved.

No part of this book may be reproduced, stored in a retrieval system, or transmitted in any form or by any means electronic, mechanical, photocopying, recording or otherwise, without the prior written permission of the publishers and author.

ISBN:1523749113
ISBN-13: 978-1523749119

Acknowledgements.

My boundless gratitude goes out to The Ladies Wot Read. Fiona Foley for her comprehensive and kind assistance spotting bloopers, Alison Mary Appleton-Brown for her encouragement, Gail Turpin for her design work and her belief that there was more to the Dust Bunnies than just dirt.
Also I'm deeply indebted to Richard Erlac for his sterling work transforming ugly .docs into swans.

Dedication

To my wife Freda without whom I'd still have
my head down in the dirt.

RAYON THE DUST BUNNY AND A VACUUM ABHORRED

CHAPTER 1

Josh got the morning wrong. He looked outside, saw snow heaped in piles, and dressed to keep warm. Somehow, though, Josh hadn't taken into account a sky full of accompanying sunshine. So, when he did step outside to leave for his friend Andrew's house, Josh was braced for a sharp, snowball-to-the-face kind of cold.

He was welcomed instead by a big warm smooch from an early springtime sun and an engulfing embrace of soft air. As he trudged through and around the melting snow piles on his way to Andrew's house, Josh - whether through laziness or a keen lack of situational awareness - kept his favourite hat pulled down tight and his jacket done up snug while this unexpected gift of solar warmth sneaked through his winter wear and warmed his bones. By the time he reached Andrew's house, Josh was over-heating vigourously.

Josh, red-faced, soggy, sweaty but only slightly whiffy, bellowed his hellos to Andrew's mum as the pair of them plodded upstairs to the sanctuary of Andrew's room. Josh tugging at the zip of his jacket to let the steam out.

Flopping down on the bed in Andrew's room, Josh pulled at the slightly soggy hat clinging to his very sweaty head. This rough handling of the well-worn and grimy outer edges of Josh's hat finally severed the last remaining thread anchoring a small, tightly-coiled bundle of fibres to the fabric of the hat. As this thread broke and recoiled back into its native warp and weft, a small and as-yet-still-insignificant ball of blue hat fluff, blue as the sky outside, was cast adrift into mid-air and the arms of gravity.

That ball of blue hat fluff was Rayon - named, as all dust bunnies are at first - after the thread of which it was made.

As Rayon tumbled backwards into the void, he saw for the very first time in his manufactured existence the hat of which, until that very instant, had been his home. The hat from whence he came was still clinging tenaciously to a large hairy lump of a thing currently making *nnnh nnnh* noises. The hat and its grunting contents were sitting atop a larger formless mass, the limbs of which were tugging at the hat energetically, but not very productively.

Ohhh, thought Rayon, his view expanding as he fell, *so that's The Josh. I've only ever seen his spotty neck. And look, there's the other one, just like him.*

This, Rayon knew, was The Andrew, The Josh's friend, and this must be the place where the bigger lumps (who tended and fed The Andrew) kept him when the bright went away. Hat finally off, The Josh now wrestled his way out of a jacket that fought back with a damp and clammy tenacity. All this sleeve-flapping engendered localised turbulence that wafted Rayon upwards, practically to the ceiling, higher than the light bulb, and flipped him over so he could see what lay below.

Around the top of the light bulb, where nobody ever looked and only the lightest and most delicate of fluff ever reached, lacey clusters of pristine white, almost luminous light bulb dust bunnies watched Rayon's slow trajectory. They politely cheered and waved as he floated past, so Rayon waved a thread or two back as a show of good manners.

With his trajectory peaking at the lightshade, Rayon started his descent. This was not a gut-wrenching, unstoppable-meteoric-plunge kind of fall, with a thud or a bang at the end, because dust bunnies are too flimsy for that kind of ballistic tomfoolery except when wet. Instead, Rayon descended from the ceiling in a relaxed, spiralling, bobbing meander aided and assisted by the last of The Josh's wafts and up-draughts.

A few random but persistent vortices tugged at Rayon. Even

while dwindling in strength, these mean little twists of air threatened to take Rayon spiralling down in ever decreasing circles to the bottom of a well of still air, somewhere over-looked, over-crowded and dismally uninteresting. A sad, back-of-a-desk, behind-a-filing-cabinet kind of place.

But The Wind was kind to Rayon this time. The Andrew, recoiling violently from the sudden release of fresh, warm Josh fumes, stirred up a swirl, drawing Rayon back from the boundary layers where the vortices lurked, and back into the major currents, right back into the swim of things.

Oblivious to his good fortune, Rayon floated aroundwards and downwards, scanning the room from horizon to horizon, his dust bunny instincts assessing his new surroundings. *So, lightshade, walls, ceiling, floor. Definitely indoors then. Bonus. No wind, no rain, low UV - that's an improvement.*

Rayon read the signs of a lingering untidiness all around him. Up here, at the higher altitudes, Rayon drifted past cliff faces stacked with shelving; ledges laden to overspill with jagged drifts of shining, almost luminous displays of fractured shapes and colour. These were The Andrew's abandoned toys - the defunct, the scuffed, the cracked, the deliberately mutilated and the no-longer coveted. There were mounds of bright plastic parts, long separated from their kin, scattered bits of puzzles and games liberated from their boxes and random, torn pages of badly-drawn and badly-coloured-in pictures submerged under logjams of desiccated felt pens, pointless pencils and crumbling crayons.

Looking down, Rayon saw a vast, sprawling delta of messiness reaching to the walls, a morass of unsorted clothes, underwear best left undescribed, orphaned socks, escaping T-shirts and badly-behaved bedsheets.

Lovely, thought Rayon as he surveyed the slowly approaching floor, or what little he could see of it. *Barely a hint of tidiness to be seen. I think I'll like it here.*

Below him, The Josh and The Andrew had stopped stirring up the atmosphere and settled on the bed in order to ignore each other while playing games that go 'beep'.

Rayon landed with barely a buckled thread, alone in a wasteland of slightly grimy beige carpet far from everything. It may have been just a regular-sized bedroom, but to Rayon, down there on the floor, it was a vast, sprawling and towering cavern, a cave so big you'd get very tired running towards any one of the walls.

Looking up from the middle of it all, the lightshade he'd floated past earlier seemed as far away to him now as the sun was when he was outside. High up, the walls were papered with vivid rectangular patches of colour overlaid with some kind of scribbling that looked as if it meant something. To his right was the bed, thrust out into the room, unscalable, massive. It made him dizzy when he tried to tilt back a bit to see the top of its towering solidity. High like the clouds, big like a continent.

Ahead, lofty elegant chair legs soared upwards to prop up sprawling wooden platforms that seemed to be collection points for the clothes that dangled over the seat edges in long, swooshing drapes and swathes; waterfalls and ocean waves of fabric that looked, to Rayon, about to fall to the floor at any minute. To his left, a mountainside of open drawers seemed to cast the deepest, longest, most secure-looking shadows. However, the bed was closer, so Rayon heaved a sigh, gave a puff and started rolling, wondering if the natives would be friendly.

As Rayon came to a rest closer to the bed, a mostly white-ish dot shot out from the shadows under the bed with a cross squeak, bounced twice and started to roll towards him. Rayon considered it rude to simply stand there, so he started rolling again, too. As the slightly white dust bunny rolled closer and closer, Rayon noticed a strange sensation that was making his fibres tingle madly and stand on end. A few more revolutions later and he had just enough time to think *Wa! Hoo! Ah!* before he was plucked by forces beyond his control to find himself clinging to the blonde, ivory and white threads of a startled, indignant and very-much-less-than-happy blonde dust bunny.

While their fibres weren't exactly what could be described in polite company as 'entwined', they were so close enough together it would be hard to tell the difference without a magnifying glass. They were practically mingling and without so much as a proper introduction.

'Sorry. Static electricity,' spluttered Rayon after he found where he'd left his senses.

'You don't have to hold on quite so tight, you know.'

'Sorry, can't help it. You are very attractive.'

'I'm told I have loose electrons,' said the dust bunny, trying unsuccessfully to peel herself from Rayon. As soon as she got one of her threads loose, it just whipped over to cling to another of Rayon's.

'Electrons! Were there sparks?'

'Not for me.' She gave up struggling against Rayon's persistent clinging. 'Knickers.'

'Well, I'm not too pleased about this myself.'

'No. Me, you fuzzball. Knickers.'

'Is a name?' tried Rayon.

'Correct. Gusset stitching, pearlescent lacey trim and elastic. You?'

'Rayon. Ex-hat. Treated cellulose. Recently entangled. Pleased to meet you.'

'You must come with me to somewhere less visible.'

'But I only just got here.'

'You're very bright and yet dim at the same time, aren't you? You are so blue. If this room didn't have a lid on it, you could be seen from space. Come on, puff and aim for the bed.' Knickers tutted. 'It'll take ages to get us tweezed apart. I hate being tweezed.'

'Why you?' asked Rayon as they rolled in the general direction of the welcoming perpetual twilight under the bed.

'Why me what?'

'Why did you come out to get me?'

'I was sent.'

'Sent?'

'I was told to come out and get you.'

'You were told to come and get me?'

'Yes, because right now,' explained Knickers, 'we really need a dust bunny who repeats everything we say in the form of a question. "*Get that luminous lump out of sight before The Mum sees it.*" they said. Before I had a chance to speak, they all puffed at once and here I am in an unasked-for, high voltage static electric clinch with a dust bunny of questionable fibre. This is all because I'm just underwear to them. They don't care about me.'

'Who's they?' asked Rayon.

'They're the Biddies, of course. That lot.'

Knickers prised away a thread from Rayon's electrostatic grip and waved it towards the clumps of dust bunnies watching their approach from under the bedgloom. Rayon could see ranks of dust bunnies, lining every nook and cranny in the clutter under the bed and all around the trench where the carpet met the wall.

'Yes, meet the Biddies,' said Knickers. 'A bit of this and a bit of that. I should warn you - they're dreadful materialists.'

Knickers and Rayon came to a stop right in front of the unwelcoming committee of the dust bunny tribe from under the bed.

'What rarely-inspected chemical factory do you think he spilt from then?' said one.

'Oh, he's synthesised or I'm not real wool,' said another.

'Is that colour allowed? My eyes, my eyes.'

'And what's he doing with our Knickers? The proximity!'

RAYON THE DUST BUNNY AND A VACUUM ABHORRED

The bedroom dust bunnies were lined up, staring at Rayon like curious cows and laughing. *Nice to meet you too*, thought Rayon.

'Just ignore them,' tutted Knickers. 'They're a bit snagged and twisted in these parts.'

Rayon could see the bedroom tribe were a drab lot. Browns of every shade of mud, yesterday's salad greens, cheerless greys of rainy days, weary pastels, blotchy blues, mottled whites. After his time on the hat, Rayon couldn't believe how unexciting and dismal their colours were.

Another voice piped up from under a nearby shoe.

'One hundred per cent unnatural fibres, guaranteed. Do you think he's a fire risk?'

'Fresh from an oil refinery. Smell the hydrocarbons; he may spontaneously combust.'

Rayon had a hard job shouting back furiously over the laughter.

'I am not a synthetic oil-based by-product,' he replied. 'Just because my molecules have been dissolved, immersed, squeezed flat, dried, shredded, oxygenated, carbon-disulfided, crumbled, ripened, filtered, de-gassed, extruded, dyed and woven before I got here, I'm still cellulose at heart. And so are any of you with cotton in your threads.'

'But we don't glow in the dark, mate.'

Rayon began to say, in a stern way, that he did not glow in the dark, but he knew he'd never be heard over the laughter now.

'See? I told you they were like that,' said Knickers. 'Don't get knotted, they're not worth the loops. The designer label crowd are worse, though, but they don't mix with us common-or-garden types. Ssh! What's that?'

The laughter had stopped abruptly and so had the abuse.

'Why's everyone gone quiet?' piped up Rayon.

Knickers shushed Rayon again.

'Quick, look like inanimate matter.'

Glancing around, Rayon noticed that all the dust bunnies under the bed now looked just like random bits of fuzz and threads.

'How'd they do that?' asked Rayon, who was still a very fresh dust bunny and not fully versed in the ways of the world.

'Shut up and go floppy,' hissed Knickers. 'And listen.'

Rayon went floppy and felt the floor shaking before he heard or saw anything. Rayon could tell from the slow bumping and heaving noises that something was hauling itself up the stairs.. The door was thrown open and The Wind rushed in first, sending the Biddies scuttling for the low-pressure areas, but leaving Rayon and Knickers alone and highly visible at the edge of the bed. Behind The Wind came The Mum. Furry green slippers appeared at the door and stopped. Towering above was a gigantic blimp of pink dressing gown, a cumulonimbus of shining folds and shadowy billows filling the room with its satiny loveliness.

'That's The Mum,' Knickers whispered to Rayon. 'She hasn't been in here in a while. Her new human is almost ripe, apparently. They grow from the inside out, you know.'

'You, creature,' squawked The Mum pointing at The Josh. 'Get downstairs with those wet shoes. Now! Off that bed, off those clean sheets, off this floor, off your feet. No, don't march back downstairs again; take your wet boots off right here and then carry them downstairs. You'll find the way, just go in the opposite direction to the wet muddy footprints you left on the way up.'

The Josh turned his slow, blinking gaze to the floor, only now noticing the last of the slush disappearing into the carpet and the darker patch of damp around his boots.

'Oh.'

'Yes, oh. Now go-oh. Before there's a hideous slaughter-oh.'

The Josh lumbered off the bed, boots in hand.

'I'm sorry, Mrs C. I'll tidy it up.'

'Paper towels are under the sink in the kitchen. Bring the whole roll and start at the bottom and work upwards.'

As The Mum stepped into the room and The Josh went out, he had just enough time to look back and catch The Andrew's eye and pull his best ogre face at him. Buckling under the strain of suppressed agony, The Andrew tried very hard not to die laughing as The Mum went on.

'Look at this place! It's barely fit for human habitation and it smells like something vultures would turn their noses up at.'

'Vultures have beaks, Mum.'

It was the ensuing silent treatment that made The Andrew crack.

'All right, I submit, I submit. I'll tidy up.'

'Your aunt arrives soon and I don't want her thinking this branch of the family tree lives in a horse's nest. And get that aromatic laundry downstairs and your clean clothes back up here and put away. Game off. Go.'

'But I've just got to Level Four,' replied The Andrew.

'Well, if it's a game you want, I'll give you a game. You get food, clothing and lodging when you obliterate these.'

The Mum looked down to the carpet, scanning for something to use as an example.

'Ha!'

And with that, Rayon looked up in mounting horror as The Mum started to lean towards him and Knickers. The Mum loomed over them, obliterating all light except for a vague pinky glow. Just when he thought he was going to be crushed, gigantic fleshy pincers with bright red talons popped out of the dressing gown sleeve and plucked Rayon and Knickers up from the floor.

Rayon had only a rough idea of what the words 'brandished aloft' meant, but having it done to him soon cleared up any ambiguity. It was like being pinched hard all over, whizzed up to an impossible height, spun around and waved about from side to side by something you knew did not feel well-disposed towards you at all.

With Rayon and Knickers firmly pinched between thumb and forefinger, The Mum was waving them within inches of The Andrew's face. Rayon didn't have the words or ideas to make sense of what he saw, but the words *potato* and *dough* came to mind. The Mum was explaining the rules of the new game.

'Your planet is infested with invaders, just like this one,' continued The Mum still waving Rayon and Knickers about, their threads bending this way and that with the speed of it. 'Millions are waiting to be dispatched by the ultimate weapon, the central vacuum cleaner.'

'That is so tragic,' grumbled The Andrew.

The waving stopped, but Knickers and Rayon were still pinched tightly between gigantic finger and thumb.

'Too bad,' replied The Mum, 'participation is mandatory. It's tidy-up time. Acquire skill, deploy central vacuum cleaner.'

'Aww, Mum.'

'No "aww Mum". Go. Do. Now. Or no eat.'

'Oh, all right,' said The Andrew in his best sullen voice and he rolled off the bed with the pace and mass of a geological event.

As The Mum turned to follow, she gave a flick of the wrist and a snap of her fingers and Rayon and Knickers were cast with extreme prejudice onto the vagaries of The Wind.

Despite the bustling departure of The Mum and The Andrew, and the subsequent massive displacement of air from the closing door, The Wind wasn't too capricious and merely stirred Rayon and Knickers around the room a few dozen times, making them dizzy, before dumping them back on the floor, this time closer to a chair near the door. With the static electricity between them finally spent, Knickers peeled herself away, thread by thread, from Rayon's lingering clinginess. It was very much quieter with the people gone, with only The Josh's game beeping forlornly on the bed.

'I'd never seen a whole people before now. They're so thick and dense you can't see through them at all,' said Rayon.

'They all look the same to me,' said Knickers. 'Although they do smell different from time to time, I can tell you. Now, where did The Wind dump us this time?'

Just as Rayon and Knickers looked around to get their bearings, a stern voice called to them from the general direction of a chair leg.

'Attention, dust bunnies in target zone. Vacate the area immediately. Compliance imperative.'

'That sounded very important,' said Rayon to Knickers. 'I wonder what it means?'

'It came from over there,' said Knickers waving a thread towards the chair, 'but I can't see anybunny.'

'Message repeats. Evacuate local vicinity immediately. Impending jeopardy levels high.'

'Yes,' agreed Rayon, 'it's definitely coming from over there. It sounds bossy, but I don't understand what it wants us to do.'

An angry voice drifted over to them.

'Oh, for crying out loud. Stour, you talk to them and get those civilians under cover.'

'Yes, sir. Oi, you two dizzy pellets! Stop gawping and get yourselves over here.'

Rayon had never been called a pellet of any kind before, but he was pretty sure he wasn't being complimented. Knickers obviously understood the sentiment more thoroughly.

'Who are you calling a pellet, you granny knot?' Knickers shouted back towards the chair.

'Contact established, sir,' came the voice from near the chair leg.

'Good work, Stour. Now get the parties in question to re-deploy to a secure area.'

'Oi, pellets. Get over here,' called out Stour.

'Why? This is the only place I've been so far that hasn't been actively hostile towards me. I like it here,' shouted Rayon in reply.

'They decline to comply, sir.'

'Directive denial. Hmm.' There was brief pause, then the bossy voice gave another instruction.

'Stour, rapid R&E mission protocols enabled. Go.'

Rayon and Knickers watched as a scruffy, unkempt dust bunny rolled out from the gloom of the chair leg shadow towards them. Fibres, obviously snagged from all kinds of different fabrics, all lengths, some straight, some curly, jutted out all over the place. It was drab, too. Mostly brown and green, old tree colours. Rayon wondered if it was just jumped-up pocket lint. When it got up close, Rayon noticed it smelt funny, too. A folded-when-damp smell – not quite unpleasant, but there was quite of lot of it.

'Hello, I'm Stour, mostly army surplus gear and bits of the great outdoors. Bits of me have seen action, you know.'

Not any washing and rinsing action, thought Rayon to himself, catching another whiff of Essence de Stour.

'Rayon, ex-hat of the blobby one,' said Rayon waving a thread hello. 'This is Knickers. From over there.'

'How do.' Knickers bobbed a curtsey in greeting and moved slowly upwind.

'Charmed, I'm sure,' said Stour. 'Come on, you two. I'm on an R&E mission. We have to make ourselves scarce.'

'Wait, what's an arrendee mission?' asked Rayon.

'Recovery and extraction.'

'That sounds nothing like arrendee,' replied a baffled Rayon.

'It's the initials – the letter R for recovery and the letter E for extraction. R and E. It's an acronym. We're very fond of acronyms in our line of work. So much quicker than lengthy explanations. So can we R&E now, please?'

'Recovery and extraction of what?' asked Rayon moving on to the next large, blank space in his understanding.

'You two,' replied Stour. 'We have to get you two out of sight and somewhere safe. You heard, The Andrew will be back with apparatus soon.' The scruffy one held out a thread to Knickers.

'Grab hold?'

'He's right,' said Knickers to Rayon. 'We should go with him.'

Rayon couldn't think of any sensible reason to stay where he was, so he snagged on to the thread offered by Knickers and all three started rolling back to the chair leg.

'Come on, put some puff into it,' Stour told them. 'We'll have to find a spot for you before any tidying starts.'

'Who was that shouting at us?' asked Rayon as Stour steered them towards the shadowy hollows and carpet craters around the chair legs.

'That would be Twill. He's officer material. Keeps us regular dust bunnies out of harm's way around here. He wants you two out of sight before you attract any more attention.'

'So why didn't the bossy one say that in the first place?'

'He thought he did,' said Stour. 'He's almost opaque, you know. Picked up a lot of useful matter on his tours. He's been outdoors. Seen weather, he has. I've been around the house a while and I haven't met many dust bunnies that can say that.'

Rayon was about to mention his years on the perimeter of The Andrew's winter hat, but Stour kept on going.

'There's even gold braid somewhere.'

Arriving under the cover of the chair, Stour stopped tugging at Rayon's fibres and all three rolled to a halt. A large, densely-tangled and very well-groomed dust bunny with hints of gold braid, navy blues and khaki rolled forward to meet them. Not a fibre was out of place. Stour turned around and snapped up a thread in a tidy salute, the effect only slightly diluted by clusters of wayward threads springing up on his head.

'Stour reporting with said pellet, sir. Technically plural pellets, sir.'

'Stop calling us plural pellets,' snapped Knickers.

'All right, all right. Don't get frayed and knotted. Sir, presenting Rayon and Knickers. Previously known as the aforementioned plural pellets, sir.'

'A1 work, Stour. Another mission accomplished.'

'Thank you, sir.'

Twill rolled over to Rayon, looked him up and down and side to side, then rolled once all the way around him. 'You, dust bunny Rayon, de-brief me ASAP on your pre-mission tactical deployment parameters.'

Rayon had to think about that for a moment before replying. 'Sorry, I only got the *"You, dust bunny Rayon"* bit. The rest of it...' Rayon could only shrug.

'He wants to know who you are and how you got here and when,' said Stour.

'Couldn't he just say that?'

'Well then, it wouldn't be proper form. So...' prompted Stour, 'when, who, how?'

'I just got here, minutes ago. I fell off a hat, got zapped by Knickers' loose electrons. The Mum threw us both about, then The Wind dumped us here. I didn't know I was in the wrong place. There weren't any signs. And who are you, anyway?'

'Yes,' joined in Knickers, 'I've been about a bit and I haven't seen you around before.' She put a funny emphasis on the 'you' that made Rayon think she was a bit disappointed by the lack of previous acquaintance.

'Name is Twill, senior dust bunny of this locale. You haven't seen us before because we've adopted a permanent low profile recognition avoidance posture.'

Twill waved a thread. Rayon and Knickers watched where the carpet met the wall and a long, thin, horizontal line, no thicker than smoke, seemed to rise, thicken, and then come to life. Quiet ranks of dust bunnies manifested all along the wall, from behind the shoe boxes stuffed under the chair, around the chair legs and mostly behind the door and all the way back to the hinges. Although densely packed, the dust bunnies were silent and the junior bits of fuzz who tried to wave at Knickers were made to behave quite severely. Twill waved a thread again and the tribe near the door sank back down out of sight and, hopefully, out of mind.

'We keep our heads down low,' translated Stour.

'A low profile is our primary tactic for long-term viability.' Twill explained. 'You see, unlike those dense clustering biddies under the bed, we believe in discretion; no clumping or rolling in daylight hours. I've assumed operational command for maintaining untidiness around here and I don't want you getting us swept up. We've established a salient of entrenched untidiness here in the last few weeks and I intend to keep it that way.'

'How? By tidying us away into a darkened corner?' asked an indignant Rayon.

'Well, you haven't been here five minutes and you've already invoked the wrath of The Mum and the threat of a cleaning,' said Knickers. 'He does have a point. And he is so dense and smart-sounding.'

Rayon slumped and sighed. 'I'm just freshly entangled. This is all so new to me.'

Stour put a friendly fibre round Rayon.

'It's nothing personal, it's your colour. You're just a bit obvious, mate. Motes like you set off the compulsive tidiers no end. They'll be about you with all manner of vile instruments – brushes, dusters, mops, damp cloths, anti-static cloths, aerosols and sprays, 1500-watt vacuum cleaners. They want you gone and they have the technology to do it. I've seen whole rooms sucked clean of dust bunnies in minutes and the air smelling fresher than a citrus-scented, pine-fresh sea breeze blowing across summer meadow flowers. Horrible, horrible. All that barren neatness.'

Twill directed Rayon and Knickers towards the dent in the carpet made by the chair leg.

'Let's get you two billeted down.' He looked over at Rayon. 'Somewhere dim would be optimal. Stour, keep them on the dark side of the chair leg. In the event of turbulence, stay low and snag on tight to whatever carpet you can grab. Loops are best.'

'Ooh, he is good though, isn't he?' said Knickers admiringly. 'And so well-groomed. I can barely see a misplaced thread.'

Her threads went all a-flutter and, with Rayon explaining to Stour about Knickers' loose electrons, they rolled into the comforting dimness. Knickers looked back, reluctantly leaving Twill keeping watch from the base of the chair leg nearest the door.

In the carpet trenches around the chair leg, clusters of dust bunnies shimmied over obligingly, without any snarky colourist comments, to let Rayon, Knickers and Stour squeeze in and settle down low. Murmured introductions were made left and right, then silence settled over them.

RAYON THE DUST BUNNY AND A VACUUM ABHORRED

CHAPTER 2

Just when it was all snug and quiet, Rayon heard a voice arching high and clear over the silence.

'The Wind that blows backwards is coming!'

'Not now, Pure. This isn't the time,' shouted out a neighbour of Rayon's and Rayon turned to see who he was yelling at.

Clearly visible, way out beyond the security of the chair legs, was a creamy white, pristine dust bunny, lightly fluffed within, more translucent than transparent. She was a wisp of a thing, threads teased out into shades of white and light and without a particle of dust clinging to her.

'Pure, commence immediate return to secure position.' Rayon recognised Twill's bossy voice calling out, but the message wasn't getting through to Pure.

'Vortices! Vortices! Fan death in a tube!' cried Pure to the ceiling.

Pure was rolling out towards the dangerous reaches, far beyond the chair's forelegs; a region feared and avoided by sensible dust bunnies for its lack of cover, low snagging opportunities and glaringly high visibility in the face of a hostile tidy-up. There she span and tumbled in a loose circle, wailing about mass displacement, the tubes and, woe, the nozzle.

Rayon nudged his neighbour and pointed at Pure. 'What's she talking about? And isn't it dangerous out there?'

'That's Pure,' explained Rayon's neighbour. 'She's one hundred per cent pure unbleached organic fair trade cotton, but her name shrank to Pure. Seeing how she's closer to a natural state and all, she has visions. She's a lovely bunny, but oddly woven.'

'But what's she talking about?' asked Rayon.

'And an unnatural Wind shall turn against us and lay low the realm of the dust bunnies,' wailed Pure.

'It's generally hard to tell until afterwards,' said Rayon's neighbour. 'She tends to be light on specifics. Doesn't sound good, though, does it? Oh, she's off again.'

'Bow to centralvac, HooverDysonElectrolux, greater cleaning power, flexibility and no pesky cords.'

At that moment, the bedroom door banged open and The Andrew barged in, wrestling several meters of unwieldy black tubing, as thick as his wrist, into his room. Having been thrown to the floor, the coils of the central vac lay dark and silent.

There wasn't a bedroom dust bunny that wasn't paying rapt and mute attention as The Andrew searched amongst the coils for what the dust bunnies knew to be the tail.

'What in the name of all that is manufactured is that?' asked a startled and not-a-little-nervous Rayon.

'That's the central vac, that's what that is,' replied his neighbour. 'All you can do now is stay low and hang on tight. Don't do anything brave. You'll know when it's over – you'll either still be here or you'll be somewhere very, very dark.'

Rayon and the dust bunnies watched as The Andrew triumphantly pulled up an end of the tube and thrust it into a receptacle in the wall. Through the floor and through the air, Rayon sensed something starting. A light wind was stirring now, getting faster.

Twisting in circles to unravel the hose, the unseeing, unthinking rear-end of The Andrew bumped into the chair by the door, nearly toppling it, but the chair leg came crashing back down, trapping Pure by her longer threads. Pure didn't seem to notice. With her threads starting to flap in the increasing air current, she still managed to point an accusatory thread at the central vac.

'It comes, it comes! A plague on its laminar flow, a pox on its turbulence. Curse its pressure gradients!' cried Pure. 'Vile

RAYON THE DUST BUNNY AND A VACUUM ABHORRED

Corryvrecken of the air.'

From somewhere in the coils of tubing, The Andrew pulled out the roaring blunt, headless body of the central vac. He fitted a long black tapering snout on to the blunt end, which heightened the roaring of the vacuum cleaner to a fiercer shrieking blast. Now the blind, mindless sucking maw of the central vac had the undivided attention of the massed ranks of mute and inert dust bunnies. That unseeing, untiring, ever-inhaling head, seeking, probing, was about to reach into the remote unsullied parts other vacuum cleaners could not reach; deep, deep into the rarely-visited domain of the dust bunny.

Although pinned down by the chair leg, not even trying to pull herself away, Pure remained defiant. In plain sight and with no attempt at concealment, resolute and still declaring at the tempest, Pure railed even as the howl of the central vac reached full song.

'Maelstrom! Vortex! Inhalation!'

The Andrew had his hand around the throat of the central vac now and lowered it to the floor. The dust bunnies watched in mute horror as the screaming black head of the central vacuum swung to and fro in a slow, methodical sweep, advancing systematically across the floor from the door towards Pure.

'At least he's not using the head of the spinning brushes,' shouted Rayon's neighbour over the noise. 'It beats as it sweeps as it cleans. Just cling on and hope he's too lazy to do the job properly.'

'What about Pure?' yelled back Rayon.

'Nobunny can do anything for her now.'

The Andrew jabbed the snout of the central vac at the base of the chair leg. The central vac's suction had Pure completely in its grip now. The full force of the central vac clawed at her very fabric, tearing her apart, fraying away the extremities of even her stronger threads. Pure's looser threads were beating this way and that and some suddenly whipped away in their entirety, reducing her to an even skimpier version of herself.

Rayon could see her threads thrashing in the torrent of air, suddenly being snatched away by the teeth of the gale. She was getting smaller as he watched. Even as she faded away, Rayon could still pick out Pure's plaintive voice over the world-filling noise, crying out.

'Yarn, Yarn knows how to save us. Yarn will help us save ourselves. Yarn...'

Rayon had no idea what she was talking about. Pure's voice was drowned by the howl of the central vac and Rayon could only watch as, thread by thread, she was finally teased apart, plucked and torn into a nothing. All that remained of Pure was a few snapped and torn thread ends snared under the chair leg.

Suddenly, a new noise added to the storm. A tortured mechanical shriek screeching up the length of the central vac tubing. As quickly as he could, The Andrew dropped the snout of the central vac and yanked the tail from the wall receptacle. Over the slowly diminishing noise, The Andrew leant out of his bedroom door and bellowed downstairs.

'Mum, the vac's just died again.'

'It killed itself rather than consume your horrible sloughing debris, you mean,' said the now-bootless Josh, pushing past The Andrew back into the room. 'Can we get back to Level Four now?'

Even though Rayon and the dust bunnies were quite close to the door, they couldn't make out The Mum's muffled reply. However, they caught a sense of great disgruntlement and the words '*repair man*' and '*next week*' and '*do the job properly*' floating back up the stairs.

'Ok,' replied The Andrew and he turned back into the room. 'Yay, vac's busted 'til next week. Pass me that end.'

The Josh handed The Andrew the tail of the central vac and he coiled its tubes around himself and bashed out of the room and down the stairs, dragging the lifeless snout of the central vac behind him.

A silence settled on the room again interrupted only by The Josh making the Level Four go beep. Rayon raised himself slowly to peer over the edge of the carpet. Pure's last five threads, four and a broken bit really, now lay motionless under the chair leg.

'Where's Pure? Where's the rest of her?' Rayon asked, looking to his neighbours on both sides.

'Don't you know?' replied one neighbour, giving Rayon a worried look. 'You never seen a disentanglement before?'

'No. Like I told Twill and Stour, I only just got here. On him.' Rayon waved a thread at The Josh. 'I don't know anything yet.'

Rayon watched as Twill tentatively rolled out a few inches from his hiding spot into open space to assess what was left of Pure. He rolled back and Rayon heard him tell a fretting cluster of dust bunnies the bad news.

'Nothing. All disentangled.'

On hearing Twill's news, the cluster of dust bunnies seemed to sag and they just rolled silently away, back to somewhere safe and sound.

'Will somebunny tell me what just happened?' said Rayon, trying not to let his voice rise above a whisper.

'The central vac got here. Tidied her up, swept her away.'

'Pulled apart, Pure was, by The Wind that blows backwards.'

'Did the central vac eat her?'

'Not exactly eat.'

'Consumed, though, thread by thread. You saw that.'

'But where did she go? All Pure's entangled threads?' Rayon was having difficulty with the idea of Pure being there, then suddenly there not being a Pure at all.

'Into the belly of the central vac. Somewhere down in the basement, I've heard.'

'So she can come back?'

Rayon's neighbours fell quiet. Rayon looked to the other nearby dust bunnies as if they might have an answer.

'No, that's just it,' said one. 'Look, you don't come back after you've been disentangled. There's no more you to come back. All your threads get separated and whatever makes you you, escapes through the gaps. Now there's no more Pure. You just saw the end of Pure.'

It took a moment or two for this to sink in to Rayon's recently entangled fibres.

'So, the central vac disentangles all kinds of dust bunnies?'

'All kinds. You too.'

'Gobbles us up whole, sometimes,' another dust bunny added.

'But then there'd be no us anymore. No me. No you. Nor any of us,' said Rayon.

'That's right.'

'All tidied up,' agreed a dense nearby dust bunny solemnly.

Rayon went quiet for a while, allowing all this new information to filter further in and reach a conclusion.

'But that's horrible. Dreadful.'

Rayon had another think.

'So that's why you hide where the central vac can't reach?'

'Now you've got it,' said the dense dust bunny. 'Know your enemy. Well, now you know yours.'

'Poor Pure,' said Rayon and couldn't think of anything else to say.

RAYON THE DUST BUNNY AND A VACUUM ABHORRED

CHAPTER 3

With only The Josh beeping on the bed, Twill waved a thread and the dust bunny tribe rose from the dents and craters of the carpet and looked out at where the central vac had taken Pure. Rayon caught snatches of hushed comments around him.

'That was bound to happen one day.'

'Poor thing, she didn't have to go like that.'

'That's what happens when a dust bunny doesn't do as they're told and keep their head down,' this last comment addressed to the younger dust bunnies of the tribe.

Twill turned to address the assembled dust bunnies.

'Bedroom chair dust bunnies, although we've lost Pure to the central vac today, we're safe for the moment. You all heard The Mum – the central vac gets repaired next week. So, after a moment of silence for the passing of Pure, I'm invoking a clumping.' He peered out over the assembled murmuring dust bunnies, waiting for any objections. A sombre quietness rolled over the tribe. Nobunny spoke out.

'Very well, a moment for one hundred per cent pure unbleached organic fair trade cotton,' said Twill. After a heavy silence, Twill spoke up again. 'Clump up. It's safe for now. Come on, come on. Pull yourselves together.'

Clumping didn't happen very often in case they got spotted, so it had to be quite important if a clumping was called. Twill hitched onto a passing eddy to hoist him up onto a stranded plastic brick and was encouraging the dust bunnies at the back to move closer. Stour was rounding up the slower dust bunnies and encouraging the nervous and the timid, telling them it was all right to let go of their carpet loops and come out now.

As Twill was waiting for the bedroom chair dust bunnies to link threads and join the larger clumps, Rayon rolled over to Twill on his brick and tugged at one of his shiny gold threads.

'Excuse me, but who's Yarn?'

'Say again, young dust bunny,' said Twill, turning quickly to look down at Rayon.

'Who is Yarn?' This time he said it really slowly.

'How could you possibly know about Yarn?' asked Twill. 'I thought you were just freshly entangled ten minutes ago?'

'Yarn. She said Yarn. That dust bunny, Pure. I heard her say "*Yarn knows how to save us*" before she blew away. Who's Yarn?'

'Yarn's the dust bunny who's never been tidied up, nor ever will be,' answered Twill. 'Said to have been living in the attic since before the house was built. You did say "*Yarn knows how to save us*", didn't you?'

'No, I just heard it. Pure said it.'

'Really?'

'Really really,' confirmed Rayon. Rayon was just beginning to recognise an increasingly puzzling feeling about this Yarn and his relationship to this building. However, the thought didn't have time to ripen before Twill addressed the attentive clumped dust bunnies – a dense, impenetrable mass now, almost as thick as felt and as silent.

'Bedroom chair dust bunnies, some news. Young Rayon here tells me that Pure invoked the name of Yarn before her disentanglement.' A low surprised murmur ran over the collected dust bunnies.

'Rayon's right. I heard her, too,' piped up a voice that Rayon recognised as his neighbour in the carpet trench.

'"*Yarn knows how to save us*". That's what she said,' continued Twill. 'You all knew Pure's pronouncements; she was mostly right, eventually. This time, her last time, Pure was telling us that Yarn will know what do when The Wind that blows backwards comes.'

It took a while for this to sink into the dense mass of dust bunnies around Rayon. However, when it did, they all seemed much reassured and cheered by the invocation of Yarn's name, despite the real and pressing threat of the central vac coming back to life next week.

'We need to talk with Yarn before the repairman comes,' said Twill. 'Only a few darks remain.' He called out over the dust bunnies again. 'So, who amongst you will seek out Yarn?'

It went very quiet. Looking round him to see who'd volunteer, Rayon was surprised to see every dust bunny under the chair looking back at him. Then the assembled clump of massed dust bunnies all pointed at Rayon and cheerfully cried with one voice.

'He will, he will.'

'Well, that's settled then,' said Twill. 'All democratic and correct. Come with me, young Rayon, and we'll get you on your way to meet Yarn.' He spoke in an important announcement kind of voice and rolled off his brick to lead Rayon out from the centre of the cheering dust bunnies.

'No, no,' said Rayon, trying to shrug off Twill's tenacious grip. 'I don't even know what a Yarn is, or where to find one. I'm too new.'

Twill pulled Rayon closer with one of his stouter threads so only he could hear. 'Listen, you simple loop,' he whispered. 'If you stay here, you'll be one of the first sucked up the central vac. People always clean up the obvious stuff first. And if they get you, they'll get my tribe. Just pretend to cooperate, play along. It's not like anybunny's going to be in a hurry to follow us.'

'Where are you taking me?'

Twill shouted impatiently at the crowding clumps of aggregated dust bunnies. 'Come on, make a space, make a space for our brave young Rayon. Stour there, lend a thread.'

With Twill on one side and Stour on the other, Rayon decided he could only co-operate and he let himself be led from the dense centre of the dust bunnies towards the door.

'Are we going to see Yarn right now?' asked Rayon, his threads barely touching the floor.

'Not exactly,' said Twill, 'but this looks like we're expeditioning and being intrepid and that's the important thing. This'll keep the tribe from migrating off somewhere until we get back. Come on, put a bit of puff in it, we don't want to be out here all day.'

Twill and Stour had to more or less drag Rayon across the featureless swathe of carpet to the only oasis of shelter, the relative safety of a shoebox dropped near the door. As they rolled into the shadows of the shoebox, Rayon asked in a hushed voice, 'Is this where Yarn lives?'

'Oh no,' replied Twill as they came to a halt. 'Right, we'll stop here and re-group. Stour, I think we can unravel ourselves from young Rayon now. Signs of anything untoward?'

'No, sir,' said Stour. 'All humans currently accounted for. All dust bunnies present and correct.'

'No, wait, wait. Not at all correct,' interrupted Rayon. 'If this isn't where the Yarn is, then where is he?'

'Right now? Couldn't tell you,' replied Stour.

'And at any other time?' said Rayon, pressing the matter.

'Couldn't tell you then, either,' answered Twill.

'So neither of you have a clue how to find Yarn?'

'Correct,' answered Twill.

'But I thought we were going to see this Yarn?'

'And so we are.'

'But you just said you had no idea how to find this Yarn.'

'Indeed, I did.'

'Then how will we find him?'

'Just because I don't know how to find Yarn precisely at this instant, doesn't mean I shall never know how to find Yarn, does it?'

said Twill.

'No,' said Rayon after thinking a bit. 'I suppose you're right. It's not very reassuring, though.'

'We shall accumulate operational intelligence,' explained Twill in a conciliatory way.

Rayon's blue seemed to brighten perceptibly. 'That sounds good. What does that mean?'

'We figure out what to do as we go along,' said Stour.

A shout from downstairs about a drink and something to eat lured The Josh away from Level Four and out the room. In the freshly hatched silence left by his departure, Rayon looked out across the floor. Where there was once just carpet, now there was movement, a shimmering. Displaced dust bunnies on the move, heading home or finding a new one. Groups of experienced and dense dust bunnies were gently shepherding herds of small, tightly-rolled dust bunnies, entangled just a few minutes ago from the boys' socks, away from the wild open spaces of the bedroom floor into the nice, dark bits underneath the dresser.

Homing instincts and slowly rotating air currents ushered generously proportioned sports gear dust bunnies and bouncy sweater dust bunnies back to their usual roosting sites, where they gave a little wiggle and settled down, if not out of his sight, then certainly out of The Andrew's mind. Within a minute or two, the bustle of activity slowed, then stopped and all looked normal again – fuzz and fibres in every niche, nook, cranny, crevice, indentation, recess and notch.

Out here, near the door, far from the walls, Rayon noticed how much space there was in front of him, behind him, on each side of him and above him. Rayon hadn't minded big, open spaces when he was up there, part of a hat; down here, however, on the floor, he felt small, insignificant and exposed.

Looking back wistfully to the inviting gloom under the chair and all that comforting debris, Rayon saw that all the dust bunnies had vanished from sight. The entire tribe were just a vague grey fuzz at carpet level again.

All the dust bunnies, that is, but one. Rayon had to peer hard to make it out. Emerging from the shadows, a whitish dust bunny was bobbing towards them.

Rayon tugged at Stour and pointed a thread. 'Look, isn't that Knickers?'

Stour had to stare a while, too. 'Aye, it's her. What's she doing exposing herself like that?'

Rayon could make out Knickers waving a wayward thread.

'What do you think she wants?' asked Rayon.

'Knotted if I know,' replied Stour. 'Sir, Knickers approaching from the south-west.'

They could hear a faint voice now. 'Wait for me. Wait for me.'

'Very well,' said Twill. 'Let's hear what she has to say.'

After much vigorous puffing on Knickers' part, she bobbed and hopped her way over the irritatingly snaggy carpet to join Twill, Stour and Rayon under the shoebox.

'Wait for me,' she gasped.

'We already did,' said Stour. 'In fact, we still are.'

'Yes,' said Twill, 'what do you want?'

'Yes,' said Rayon, 'we're waiting.'

Knickers snapped a bit of elastic at Rayon.

'Ow! What's that for?' asked a smarting Rayon.

'Joining in,' explained Knickers to Rayon. 'I want to come with you.'

'Why would you want to do that?' said Rayon. 'This pair dragged me here as an act of everybody's will but mine. And they don't have a clue how to find your blessed Yarn.'

'Because I'm not sticking around with those dense clustering biddies under the bed a moment more,' said Knickers. 'They're thick as wet felt. Even though they might look every shade of pleasant, the niceness got bleached out of them long ago. Besides,' she said to Twill and Stour, 'I know how to find Yarn and you don't.'

CHAPTER 4

'We have to ride the laundry cycle,' explained Knickers to Twill, Stour and Rayon as they clustered in the temporary safety of the shoebox near the door. 'That's the only way to reach the top of the house where Yarn's supposed to be.'

'But the laundry's contra-indicational to mission objectives,' objected Twill.

'Is that good or bad?' asked a slightly baffled Knickers.

'Bad,' explained Stour. 'We'd be going the wrong way. Two lots of stairs' worth of wrong way. Down to the basement. We're supposed to be going up.'

'Yes,' persisted Knickers. 'Up on the laundry cycle.'

'What!' squawked Stour. 'Pre-soak, wash and rinse? Maybe even bleach, if his whites are anything to go by. No thanks, I don't want to end my days in a lint trap.'

'No, no, no. That's just it,' explained Knickers slowly. 'We don't need the wash cycle. We hitch a lift on the drier cycle.'

'And end up as fluffy lint instead of flat lint? In what way is that an improvement?' replied Stour.

'Would you prefer being in the belly of the central vac? In bits. Like Pure?'

It was then they felt the ponderous tread of The Andrew coming up the stairs and heard The Mum's order to separate the whites from the colours.

'Humph, colourist,' muttered Knickers under her breath. 'Look, we have to snag on now or we'll get tidied up and never get to Yarn. Let's get closer to the bed.' Knickers started rolling away from them towards the bed, but holding out a thread to grab on to.

'Twill, Stour. I know a way. Come on, Rayon.'

Rayon was torn between the sensible validity of Stour's objections and the fervent certainty of Knickers' cajoling. What to do? Follow Knickers on this laundry cycle thing or take heed of Twill and Stour's objections? With no obvious answer coming to mind, Rayon realised he had to choose for himself; to make a decision. His first.

Since he'd sprung into being fully-formed from the hat of The Josh, he'd been blown hither and yon by turbulent circumstance. But now, after being borne safely through trying times by the good graces of a benign Wind, here he was, perched at a nexus in time and space, where whatever he did or said next would most profoundly alter the course of his existence. No Wind to carry him off before he had time to think now. No Wind to make his mind up for him.

The footfall of the plodding Andrew coming up the stairs was starting to make the floor bounce ever such a little bit. Rayon had never made a decision before and he didn't like all the thinking effort choosing involved; thinking made his topmost threads buckle and fold at odd angles. He wished something – some sudden event – would happen that would make up his mind for him. Other than the ascending Andrew making the floor bounce more, nothing did.

Oh well, then, he thought to himself.

'I'm coming, too,' he heard himself say. *Funny*, Rayon immediately thought to himself, *I didn't know I was going to say that until I said it.* He started rolling after Knickers, quite pleased that the uncomfortable decision-making feeling had gone away, but a bit nervous about what was going to happen next.

Behind him, he heard Twill and Stour say a lot of cross words he didn't know the meaning of and certainly didn't like the sound of. However, when he looked back, he saw Twill and Stour grudgingly start rolling too.

'Uh oh, hold on,' said Knickers, coming to a sudden halt and causing Rayon, Twill and Stour to bash into her in a heap. 'Door's opening. Grab some carpet.'

The Andrew swept in, banging a white plastic laundry basket off the door frame before dropping it into the middle of the floor and scooping up armfuls of clothes. As The Andrew heaved his neglected laundry into the basket, Rayon, Knickers, Stour and Twill watched as drifts of dust bunnies abandoned their previously snug and secure hideaways in the heaps of clothes and hurled themselves from the rising column of clothing and onto the mercy of The Wind. It was a leap of faith, all in the hope of being carried away by a propitious zephyr or eddy to somewhere safe, rather than be compressed under the oppressive weight of laundry and a potentially one-way trip on the laundry cycle.

The wafting and waving of unwashed laundry sent knots of the luckier dust bunnies scurrying for deep cover way under the bed. Around the perimeter of the room, however, blizzards of dust bunnies were being swept this way and that by the vast billowing gusts created by the flapping Andrew.

'Come on, we have to get to the laundry basket,' said Knickers, letting a passing eddy carry her off roughly in the right direction.

'I do so hate heroics,' grumbled Twill. 'Stour, Rayon – next gust, follow that dust bunny.'

With that, Twill, Stour and Rayon unsnagged and cast themselves on the mercy of The Wind.

As it was, the laundry got them first. A dragging woolly sweater sleeve snagged Twill and Stour, but Rayon had to wait for some pyjama bottoms before he, too, was swept into the laundry basket and gently squished under layers of The Andrew's clothes, wondering what that funny smell was.

Rayon couldn't see much past a folded sock, but he felt The

RAYON THE DUST BUNNY AND A VACUUM ABHORRED

Andrew bump down the stairs, swing round corners and bump down another flight of steps. Rayon felt another thud and the sudden added weight of the laundry above compressed him notably flatter as The Andrew dropped the laundry basket to the floor.

'White, white, white,' said The Andrew. 'Colour, colour, white.'

The pressure on Rayon was lifting now and he felt himself spring back into shape. He could see patches of light above him as The Andrew reached into the basket to yank out clothes, flinging them over his shoulder into sprawling piles. Then Rayon, too, was lofted out of the laundry basket and sent spinning into the airspace of the laundry room, coming to rest near the base of a towering white edifice. Looking up, Rayon could see The Andrew force-feeding the washer his not-very-whites.

Where were Knickers, Twill and Stour? No sign of them, but the colours were still in a heap on the floor so Rayon presumed they were still tangled up in amongst The Andrew's sports gear, socks and t-shirts. A slam and a hefty click announced the starting of the washer.

Rayon instinctively flinched as the sound of a torrential waterfall came tumbling from deep within the great white block. Then the machine itself started to shake and groan. A slow grinding started, increasing reluctantly in speed and volume. Rayon heard cascades of huge volumes of tumbling water, raindrops the size of lakes, slosh and thrash ever more violently above him until the cacophony of thunderous shaking and crashing waters was all he knew. The noise, the shaking, the sound of oceans crashing on an endless wave was so much worse than the rain, wind or snow outside. Bracing for the inevitable deluge, Rayon scrunched up tight, tiny and blue at the foot of the earth-shaking washing machine, waiting for the vast sloshing storms raging above him to cascade out and sweep him away.

'What you doing?'

From somewhere under the washing machine, Rayon thought he heard a high piping voice through the deep growl of grinding thunder. Quite close.

'You're blue.' The voice was definitely closer and it wasn't a voice that sounded like it was worrying about being swept away by deluges or floods.

'What you doing?' Something was tugging at him now.

Rayon let himself unravel a bit and look around. A small ball of white fluff was looking up at him, quite unconcerned about the chaos above, holding on to one of Rayon's threads.

'Who are you?' said the ball of white fuzz.

'I'm Rayon. From a hat. You?'

'I don't know who I am yet. I rolled from there,' said the little fuzzball pointing deep into the darkness under the white mountain. 'Would you like to roll with me? I can roll. See?'

The fuzzball released Rayon and, without too much veering or hesitation, rolled right around him.

'Roll with me, roll with me,' insisted the fuzzball now back to tugging at Rayon, but without the strength to straighten any of Rayon's threads.

'I can't,' explained Rayon. 'I have to find my friends. Have you seen them?'

'Are they blue too?'

'No. Different colours.'

'I've only ever seen blue before, I probably wouldn't recognise them. Come and meet my friends. You don't have any and I have lots. Roll with me, roll with me.'

Grudgingly, Rayon admitted the tenuous little fuzzball was right. There was nothing for him here on the floor of the laundry room; the only other place to go was deep, deep under the quaking, sloshing white monolith where the fuzzballs lurked.

The overhanging darkness under the washing machine was filled with noise and seemed to go on endlessly; but then, Rayon thought he could make out a lightening of the darkness ahead. Yes, definitely a shade of dark grey ahead and getting lighter. In a lull in the mechanical storm overhead, Rayon heard the fuzzball exhorting him to roll faster. They were almost there.

Rayon and the fuzzball rolled out into the light. Not the harsh glare of the laundry room any more, but a soft grey light that ran out of brilliance, bouncing around the back of the washing machine to get this far. Although dim, there was more than enough light for Rayon to see that the walls behind the washing machine were lined with pillowy mounds of soft, creamy fuzzballs. They were banked so high up the wall that Rayon wondered why they didn't topple, given that they never stopped fidgeting and wriggling in the soft warm breeze that wafted around them.

'Are these all your friends?' asked Rayon.

'Oh yes,' replied the fuzzball. 'Or they might just be different versions of me. We're all pretty much the same as each other, so we all get along. Come and say hello.'

The fuzzball led Rayon over to the nearest wispy clump that had rolled down from the embanked heap of fuzzballs behind them.

'Hello,' said the fuzzball to his kin. 'This is Rayon and he's blue.'

'Hello Rayon,' they cried as they crowded around him.

'Have you come to roll with us? We've just rolled down from up there,' said a particularly bold young fuzzball.

'No, I've come to find my friends,' replied Rayon. 'Have you seen them anywhere?'

'Are they blue too?'

'No,' explained Rayon, 'they're bigger and darker than you, with lots of threads of different colours.' *Not just hot air*, went one of Rayon's fleeting thoughts on the matter.

'Oh, you mean like over there?' said an eager fuzzball, hopping up and down on the spot and waving a thread to show this big, but obviously dim-witted, blue dust bunny where to look.

A couple of shoe lengths away, Rayon could see Twill, Stour and

Knickers struggling to push through a deep carpet of soft white fuzzballs, clamouring for their attention as they made their way towards Rayon.

'Roll with us, roll with us.'

'I'll roll over you if you don't shut up,' grumbled Knickers as her threads got more entangled in the mat of fuzzballs.

It took Rayon, Stour, Twill and Knickers an annoyingly long time to convince the thickets of fuzzballs that they had no interest in rolling whatsoever. Eventually, the disappointed fuzzballs drifted away, leaving boring Rayon and his boring friends with only the most curious of the fuzzballs who were still paying them any attention.

'So, you've met the fuzzballs, I see,' said Knickers to Rayon.

'We're fuzzbunnies, not fuzzballs,' said one of the fuzzballs.

'You're a fuzzball until you get some proper threads of your own. Be quiet.'

'Why are there so many of them?' asked Rayon.

'They come from there,' said Knickers indicating a thick, slightly shiny grey tube further along.

'That's the drier vent,' added Stour as if that explained everything.

The drier vent was a large shiny metal tube that didn't quite fit into a hole in the wall.

'I don't understand,' said Rayon

'This lot,' said Knickers indicating the fuzzballs. 'They're escaped drier lint. They escape through that gap between the drier and the vent in their thousands.'

'Are they dust bunnies?' asked Rayon.

'Not yet. They're mostly fluffed-up lint, but some will inevitably snag a few threads of their own eventually and go on to entangle into proper dust bunnies. Meanwhile, "low thread count" if you get my meaning.'

'Not exactly.'

'Lots of volume, not much content?' offered Stour, pulling off a fervent fuzzball who had latched on firmly to his lower threads most affectionately.

'Ah.'

'You made it here all right then? All threads present? No laundry squish damage?' asked Twill.

'Other than being a bit stunned by the smell, no damage,' replied Rayon. 'Then a fuzzball brought me here. This one. At least I think it was this one.'

'Roll with me,' said another insistent fuzzball.

'Is that all they do, these wee fuzzbunnykins?' asked Stour. 'Just roll about being annoying?'

'Mostly,' agreed Knickers. 'Except when they're being useless as well. Look, we have to get going. The Andrew will be starting the drier cycle soon and we have to get on board.'

'Which way?' asked Twill.

'That way,' replied Knickers, pointing a thread at the largest, densest mound of fuzzballs under the drier vent. 'Into the heart of fluffiness.'

Rayon, Knickers, Twill and Stour made their way closer to the drier vent, clambering over the thickening milky heap of squawking fuzzballs until they were directly under the drier vent atop a mound of fuzzballs.

'What are we doing here?' asked Twill.

'Waiting for the drier to start,' replied Knickers.

'And then what?'

'All aboard the laundry cycle. Don't let go until I tell you.'

The drier starting up made a different sound to the washing cycle. Rayon could hear the air – and lots of it – was moving through the drier and he could feel it getting warmer. Much noisier too, as the drier came up to full speed and maximum heat. An endless gust of thick, hot air was now gushing up the drier vent, but also sucking in air from the laundry room through a narrow gap just above them.

'Aha! Venturi effect!' said Twill over the noise. 'I get it now. Going up!'

RAYON THE DUST BUNNY AND A VACUUM ABHORRED

CHAPTER 5

With the drier going at maximum speed, Rayon, Knickers, Stour and Twill and a clutch of fuzzballs were sucked up through the gap by the pressure differential, whisked into the warm moist mass of air and lifted into the darkness of the drier vent. Rayon floated effortlessly upwards on a powerful cushion of humid air and he could just hear Twill calling out to make sure everyone had taken off.

'You'll see a light patch soon,' shouted Knickers as they elevated upwards. 'A gap in the pipe.'

'We're going too fast,' came Stour's voice in the darkness. 'We'll end up outside.'

'Don't worry, the flow gets a bit wheezy here,' replied Knickers. 'Look, here's the gap in the tube coming up. Puff for it.'

A few well-timed and well-aimed huffs and gasps lined them up in the right position and they shot out of the poorly-fitted ventilation pipe, past the sharp edges and out into the gap between the walls. They were wafting upwards, much slower now. Above him, Rayon could see light, not much, but more than when he was looking down. As the huffing of the drier vent faded below them, Rayon could hear Knickers giving advice on the way up.

'Try not to snag on the brickwork.'

'And watch out for spider webs.'

The rising column of slow, warm air dislodged a fly corpse and it fell on Rayon, spinning him around rapidly as its passing antennae snagged ever so lightly in one of Rayon's smaller loops. When he could speak again and knew which way was up, he saw that he had fallen below Knickers, Stour, Twill and the small clutch of fuzzballs.

He could just make them out floating upwards above him, though they were hard to pick out against the faint glow. Suddenly, Knickers, Twill, Stour and the constellation of fuzzballs lit up brightly before vanishing into the black gloom without a sound or credible explanation.

Alone in the thick, dark, murky air with nothing but the faint groaning of the drier drifting up from far below him, Rayon floated slowly upwards towards the exact same place where his companions had vanished.

He saw the flash first and felt the cold air second. Tumbling over and over, he could only make out a light patch and a dark bit before landing on a hard, smooth surface and skidding some way before coming to a halt.

'No points for style. Next time, tuck and roll, tuck and roll,' offered Stour.

'Rolling and bouncing,' exclaimed a very impressed fuzzball. 'You're good. Do it again.'

Twill, Stour, Knickers and the fuzzballs watched Rayon pull his threads together.

'I should have told you about the side draught. Sorry about that,' said Knickers.

'Where are we?' asked Rayon.

'Up in the attic,' said Knickers. 'Top of the house. Like I told you we would be,' she added pointedly to Twill and Stour.

A small window set into the roof let a shaft of sunshine into the attic and Rayon could make out low mounds of things in the shadows, neat stacks of stuff and the orderly placing of objects.

'So, you come here often?' Stour asked Knickers.

'I haven't actually, precisely come here before,' replied Knickers. 'I usually snag on at the gap and wait until the drier stops, then float back down to catch the folding of the clean clothes. Smells lovely.'

'But you claimed Yarn-location-related intel,' interjected Twill.

RAYON THE DUST BUNNY AND A VACUUM ABHORRED

'What?' said Knickers.

'You said you knew where Yarn was,' translated Stour.

'I said I knew how to find Yarn. I didn't say I'd found him. I heard he was up here in the attic. Somewhere.'

'So topline the parameters of your next operational gambit for us.' requested a rather cross-sounding Twill.

Knickers looked to Stour for a translation.

'What do we do now?' he explained.

'I haven't worked that bit out yet. But we're closer, aren't we?'

The drone of the drier cycle far below slowed, then stopped and silence filled the attic. Some of the lighter fuzzballs, lofted higher than the others, were still drifting down through the beam of sunshine. Their persistent faraway cries of 'Look at me, look at me' weren't big enough to dent the growing silence and, when all the fuzzballs had landed and their faint voices faded away, there was no noise whatsoever. With nothing happening, Rayon couldn't tell if time was still passing. Then Twill spoke up and time started again.

'This won't do. Not at all. We need to find Yarn, right?'

'Yes,' said Rayon.

'But we don't know how to,' continued Twill.

'Thanks for rubbing it in,' muttered Knickers.

'No offence meant. Our objective is to find Yarn. You do agree?'

'Yes, but...'

'Right then,' said Twill, almost doubling his size with puff before letting it out at maximum volume. 'TWILL TO YARN, TWILL TO YARN, COME IN PLEASE, OVER!'

'You can't just, well, shout,' said a horrified Knickers.

'Well, for the lack of a better plan...' and Twill puffed up again. 'TWILL TO YARN! TWILL TO...'

'Stop shouting, voluminous bunny,' came a voice from the shadows behind them. 'I can hear you perfectly well.'

'Yarn?' asked a surprised Knickers.

'You were expecting someone else? Now, all of you, come over here and get out of the sunlight – it fades the colours and weakens the fibres.'

Yarn lived in the attic, in the shadows between the rafters. Around him were stacked cardboard boxes that had long lost their muscle tone and now sagged badly, old music playing systems involving some form of physical media, framed film posters, pictureless picture frames, bedside lamps seeking a shade, a unicycle with a flat tyre, and heaps of reference books from back in the days when The Mum and The Dad had things to study instead of things to worry about. Over everything, an untracked layer of dust lay like a grey cloak. That meant The Wind didn't come here often.

Dust on everything, Rayon noticed, except Yarn himself. Yarn was large, dark and dense – impenetrably so. At first glance, he looked like a dirty clump of oily, sooty dark cotton; however, when the clouds parted to let the sun shine through, enough light made it into the attic and down to the rafters to light up Yarn for a fleeting instant. For a shining moment, Yarn wasn't dark and dirty; Rayon caught glimpses of the lush deep purples from sunsets, a summer sky's lustrous blues, a forest's shadowy greens, flashes of burning autumn orange, pale pinks and yellows, mellow earthy browns and the black of wet slate.

Instead of cotton fluff and cheap fabric like the rest of the dust bunnies, Yarn was materially different. Knicker's keen eye saw Bengaline silk, chiffon, canvas, cashmere, velvet, merino, mohair, Halas lace, bombazine, cheesecloth and was that a thread of carbon fibre? *Wherever did all Yarn's threads come from?* wondered Knickers.

Every thread a story and Yarn had more threads than could be counted.

Then the sun went in and Yarn went back to being a rather dark and tatty knot of impenetrable tangles.

RAYON THE DUST BUNNY AND A VACUUM ABHORRED

'Welcome to the attic, young dust bunnies,' said Yarn as Twill, Stour and Knickers gathered round. 'Are they yours?' Yarn waved a stout, dark thread at the fuzzballs rolling each other in the dust.

'No,' said Stour. 'I think we're theirs. Or that's how they see it.'

'Hmm,' muttered Yarn. 'Fuzzballs today, with their lightweight fabrics and recycled synthetics. I take it you're not here by accident?'

'The repairman's coming,' blurted out Knickers. 'Next week!'

'I expect he is. Things do tend to break.'

'He's coming to fix the central vac, though!' added Stour.

'Oh, that old thing choked itself again, did it?'

Rayon couldn't contain himself any longer.

'But the central vac disentangled Pure,' he blurted out. 'I was right there and now they're going to mend it and The Mum's gone all tidy-uppy and wants The Andrew to clean his room and do it properly and do his laundry...' Rayon didn't pause for breath. 'Even the stuff under the bed and if we hadn't been hanging on really, really tight we would have been cleaned up, too, and when the central vac was disentangling Pure the last thing she said was to see you, because you knew...'

'Hush, hush,' interrupted Yarn gently. 'Name?'

'Yes, name,' said Rayon, trying to put the brakes on his runaway thought processes. 'Name. Aha. Yes. Rayon. Of a hat.'

'You're newly entangled, aren't you, Rayon of a hat? I discern you haven't picked up a lot of threads of your own yet, so what you must know is that this kind of thing goes on all the time. Vacuums break, vacuums get mended. Dust bunny gets entangled, another gets disentangled.'

'They do?'

'If they didn't, this house would be packed to the rafters with dust bunnies by now. No, your Pure is a victim of the Great Battle, I'm afraid. She's not the first to be disentangled and she won't be the last.'

'What's the Great Battle?' asked Rayon.

'Order versus chaos,' answered Yarn.

'Whose side are we on?' asked a fuzzball.

'Shh, don't interrupt Yarn,' whispered Knickers loudly and giving it a sharp snap with an elastic thread.

'No, the fuzzball is right to ask,' said Yarn. 'I sometimes wonder myself. Without chaos and all the mess that it entails, none of us dust bunnies would be here. Yet, without some kind of order holding us together, we'd simply fall apart. It's always hard to tell which side is winning at any particular moment, but I do know who wins in the end.'

'Oh, oh! Don't tell, don't tell,' squealed a fuzzball. 'Let us guess.'

'Quiet,' said Knickers as she rolled on top of the fuzzball. 'I'm sorry...you were saying?'

'Well,' replied Yarn, 'chaos wins in the end, of course. No contest. It's just that it'll take a while.'

'Before next week, I hope. We've got a repairman coming to fix that central vac,' pointed out Twill.

'I'm afraid things will get tidier before they get better.'

'Not when I'm around,' said Twill. 'Twill is the name. Pleased to make your acquaintance.'

He pulled himself into a neat ball and saluted with a crisp, tidy thread.

Yarn waved a thread back in Twill's general direction. 'Reciprocated, I'm sure.'

'Look...' said Twill. 'Yarn... Mr Yarn? Sir?'

'Yarn is fine. Do go on.'

'Well, we haven't had a cleaning incident for many darks and brights. The bedroom tribes are dense, plump and plentiful. There's plenty of new fluff, a steady supply of fuzzballs and we keep our heads down and stay out of order's way.' Twill flicked a thread towards Rayon. 'Or we did, until Mr Blue Sky here turned up.'

RAYON THE DUST BUNNY AND A VACUUM ABHORRED

'Somehow, I can't imagine how,' said Knickers looking very pointedly at Rayon. 'The Mum caught sight of a certain dust bunny and declared war.'

'It's not all my fault and you were there, too,' protested Rayon. 'If it were just me, the Mum would never have noticed. But you lot are so thick around the edges and dense underneath everything that you make the whole room look out of focus. No wonder she noticed.'

'Young Rayon of a hat here speaks wisely for one so newly entangled,' said Yarn. 'But there is something you need to learn. Gather closer, dust bunnies, and grasp a thread.'

The dust bunnies shuffled closer to Yarn, right up to him.

'What you must learn is this: no matter what happens next week, when the repairman comes, no matter where the brush sweeps, dust will always prevail. It always has and always will.'

When the dust bunnies touched Yarn's threads, the rafters and boxes of the dusty attic faded away. Black swirled and thickened around them. Tiny points of light began to pierce the gloom.

Oooh, space, thought Rayon to himself. *And stars, too. I've seen them up high when the bright goes away. Didn't realise it was quite so big though.*

Like strings of fairy lights, slender strands of spinning and colliding galaxies draped themselves across millions of light years of velvety darkness. Ribbons of utter black spilled across bands of light, only to be blasted away by flowering waves of light revealing a nursery of sparkling points at the centre of it all.

'This is dust at work. Making stars.' Yarn's voice rolled out across the roiling and boiling cosmos. 'Stars are the littlest bits of dust getting together to do great things.'

The dust bunnies watched as a single bright light burst into being, brighter by far than all the other stars.

'Supernova,' explained Yarn. 'Even when the dust has finished being a star, it's still got work to do.'

Becoming brighter and brighter, the star bloomed silently into an expanding translucent sphere of light and glowing dust, a star's last goodbye to the universe.

'That's what we are made of, the heart of stars rising from their ashes,' said Yarn. 'The smallest parts of our smallest fibres were forged in the heart of stars and will endure for the life of the universe.'

That was a big idea for a small dust bunny to come to terms with, so they all sat silently, slightly baffled and a bit awestruck.

'Don't take the pictures too seriously. That's all nonsense,' Yarn went on in a matter-of-fact kind of way. 'This three-dimensional, immersive, high-resolution, time-lapsed, full-colour view trick. That's just for demonstration purposes. The real universe doesn't look like that at all. Not a bit. Much, much duller in real life. So boring, so very slow.'

That rather broke the magic of the moment and Yarn's cosmos crumbled away to the very ordinary black of Yarn sitting in the shadows of the rafters in a dusty, poorly-lit attic.

Back in the reality of the attic, faced with the looming return of the central vac and a source of dubious information, Twill was exasperated. However, he did a good job of holding it in.

'Not a lot of immediate tactical relevance though, this *"forged in the heart of solar furnaces"* stuff, is it?' said Twill. 'Not much in the way of practical applications. Utility factor low.'

'Handy as a chocolate teapot,' agreed Stour.

'That cosmic starbunny twaddle. How exactly does that help us at all?' Twill's exasperation was starting to leak out a bit now.

'Oh, it's not all twaddle,' Yarn replied. 'Dust is forged in solar furnaces and tempered in the savage light and limitless heat of exploding suns uncountable years ago. We are made of resilient stuff, you and I.'

'Even me?' asked a delightedly baffled Knickers.

'Indeed so.'

This thought pleased Knickers very much and she puffed up quite conspicuously. Rayon had obviously been thinking about all this, too.

'So, from dust we come and to dust we go,' he said. 'Everything tends towards dust. Dust always prevails?'

'Exactly, young Rayon,' replied Yarn. 'Well done.'

Hearing this, Twill threw up his threads in despair and rolled away before he said something he'd later regret.

'And will dust prevail before, say, next week?' asked Stour hopefully.

'I'm afraid he's right, Yarn,' said Rayon. 'What you told us doesn't exactly help us with the central vac. What should we do?'

'Do, young bunny? Do? Any doing is quite unnecessary. Don't you fret, young dust bunnies. Dust will prevail. But perhaps not in the way you want,' said Yarn with a yawn. 'Or, indeed, in the way you expect. But yes, dust will prevail. Entropy has never failed us yet.'

Eyes closed, Yarn fell asleep, reverting back to nothing more than a largish clump of undifferentiated mung wedged against the rafters in a dingy attic.

After it became clear Yarn had nothing more to add, Twill clapped a pair of threads together and turned to the dust bunnies and fuzzballs.

'Well, that was easy,' he said. 'Let's go and prevail, shall we? Who's got the prevailer?'

'Yarn did try to help,' said Knickers. 'No need to be quite so sarcastic.'

'Oh really, how sarcastic should I be?' replied Twill. 'Let me run the executive summary of our meeting by you. There's bits, then gas, accretion disks, fusion going off, nucleo-synthesis, nova, bang, flash, elemental detritus abounds, turns into stuff, stuff turns back into dust, stars explode, back to dust again – see, everything will be fine next Tuesday. No,' he went on decisively. 'Very educational, but no situational use at all.'

'Ashtray on a motorcycle,' agreed Stour.

'So, we're moving on to Plan B,' declared Twill.

'But we don't have a Plan B,' objected Rayon. 'Do we?'

'Then let's come up with one, shall we?' suggested Twill very firmly indeed.

RAYON THE DUST BUNNY AND A VACUUM ABHORRED

CHAPTER 6

'Yarn said entropy has never failed us. What does that mean?' said Knickers.

'Well, it means entropy is reliable,' replied Stour. 'It means entropy is on our side.'

'That sounds good,' said Rayon, 'but who's entropy?'

Silence all round.

'What about the screen and monitor dust bunnies downstairs?' piped up Knickers. 'They're always telling us how clever they are, watching their television and their deevy dees and interwebs and whatnot. Maybe they know what entropy is. We could ask them. Don't expect a quick answer, though.'

'Good work, that dust bunny,' said Twill. 'We have a Plan B. Recruit entropy, whereabouts unknown. Access new intel. Location downstairs. I like the sound of it.' Twill sounded happier now he could speak in short, chopped-up sentences. Knickers was just pleased Twill liked her plan.

'Shouldn't we tell the others?' asked Rayon.

'What? About entropy?' replied Stour.

'No, about the tidy up,' answered Rayon.

'He's right,' agreed Knickers. 'The other dust bunnies deserve to know. It'll give them more time to make themselves scarce and hunker down.'

'Consolidates defensive posture,' said Twill.

Knickers and Rayon assumed he was agreeing with her.

'But how do we get word out?' asked Rayon.

'Sorted,' said Stour. 'The cack-handed Dad got in a fankle fixing a new light in the spare room. Put a hole right through the ceiling, over there. Bit of a tight squeeze, though.'

They all rolled over to take a look the hole in the attic floor. Stour was right – it was too small for any of them to get through.

'Maybe a fuzzball could get through?' offered Rayon.

'A fuzzball would get lost before it landed, then forget what it's there for,' humphed Knickers.

'Mass deployment,' countered Twill. 'Increase probability of success.'

'And we do have plenty of fuzzballs,' said Knickers, thoughtfully eyeing up her adoring throng.

With perhaps more pleasure than was appropriate, Twill, Stour and Knickers spent the next few minutes jamming protesting fuzzballs through the little hole in the attic floor. Of the many fuzzballs dispatched into the spare room, most had their simple instructions flung from their tiny minds the moment they started spinning in mid-air.

One fuzzball, however, did manage to reach the floor without forgetting his lines. The spare room dust bunnies found him dizzy and unable to roll in a straight line. However, in between the '*whees*' and the '*whoas*', he blurted out the bad news to the dust bunnies in the spare room. There was a tidy-up coming soon.

In the attic, Twill was impressing Knickers again by slowly rolling to and fro some distance away, looking serious and talking to himself in a purposeful way. Stour waited nearby for orders.

'Entropy-related intel needed,' said Twill. 'Entropy-related intel source: screen dust bunnies. Current locale of screen dust bunnies: downstairs. Downstairs access denied. Therefore, prioritise access. So, re-deploy assets to seek access. Stour!'

'Yes, sir, here sir,' said Stour. 'Got that, sir. We need to talk to the screen dust bunnies, but we're up here and they're down there, so we need to find a way down.'

RAYON THE DUST BUNNY AND A VACUUM ABHORRED

'Exactly. Pass the word around.'

'Will do, sir.' Stour rolled off to repeat to Knickers and Rayon what they'd already just heard.

Knickers hated her own idea because it meant spending time with the screen bunnies. However, she was very favourably inclined towards Twill – his decisiveness, directness and firm directions.

'Oh, he is good in a pinch, isn't he?' said Knickers after Stour explained what needed to be done. 'So purposeful and determined. And not at all scruffy,' she added, shooting a glance at Stour.

'No need to be like that. We don't get to choose what we're made of. Do we, Miss Fancypants?' said Stour pointedly. 'Now, any questions?'

'What's a screen?' asked Rayon.

'Those flat, shining things the people stare at all the time. Screens, televisions, monitors, panels – they're all the same. People can't take their eyes off them,' said Stour. 'Big screens, little screens, screens they carry about with them, screens on walls, screens they put in their pockets They all do it. Mind you, for all their non-stop gawping, they never notice the accumulating going on right in front of them. Dust bunny magnets, those television and computer screens, I tell you. No wonder – out of the reach of The Wind. Nice, gentle convection currents instead. Lots of nice warm places to snuggle down. Lots of new bits coming and going from furniture, carpets and suchlike. Bit of static electricity to keep the place attractive, too. Entertainment, sports, news, information and drama every day. Lovely. Some screen and computer dust bunnies even have their own tame Wind machine in a box. It's all very high tech.'

'Don't you want to be a screen dust bunny?' asked Rayon.

'Nah, not really,' replied Stour. 'Bit sedate for my tastes. I like a bit of adventure now and then. Proper problems to solve, not quiz questions.'

'Like "*how do we get downstairs?*"' asked Rayon.

'Exactly. Got nothing yet myself, but I'm sure Twill will come up with something.'

Behind them, they could still hear the occasional delighted squeals of the slowly descending fuzzballs, who were still being spat out from the drier vent at regular intervals.

After a while, Twill came up with a question rather than an answer. 'Knickers, any way we can ride that laundry cycle of yours downwind?'

'Can't go down against the updraught,' said Knickers. 'Too strong. Even when the hot air stops, we could only get down to the laundry room again if we could find that skinny gap in the drier vent. And it's in the dark, mind you. Even then we'd shoot past the room with all the screens and still be a flight of stairs below, where we want to be. So, in a word, no.'

'How about that gap between the walls?' said Rayon. 'It seemed to go down the same way.'

'Negatively indicated,' said Twill. 'Ascending, we had thermal up-draughts to carry us. Descending, it'd be freefall, full speed straight down. We'd be falling through a Class 5 vertical descent between those bricks. Pitch black, of course. Rough, unfinished surfaces. Snags galore. It's a vertical shredder of cross ties, wiring, piping, almost certainly abandoned larval casings, fly carcasses, spider webs – lots of opportunity to get snagged, torn or trapped.'

'Oh yes,' piped up the fuzzballs, who were clinging affectionately to Rayon's lower fibres. 'Let's not fall. Let's jump and flyyyyy all the way down. And then do it again. Flyyyyy all the way down.'

'Yes, yes, fly, we get it. Now quiet,' said Knickers. 'We need to figure out how to get downstairs in a civilised fashion. Not dented, not grated. In one piece, not several.'

'Flyyyyy all the way down, first class, welcome aboard,' sang out one persistent fuzzball. 'Please turn off any devices you may be using before landing!'

RAYON THE DUST BUNNY AND A VACUUM ABHORRED

'Travel blanket wannabe,' muttered Knickers.

For a while, there was nothing but the distant hum from the laundry. Rayon watched volleys of newly-emerging fuzzballs fluttering and wheeing their way to the attic floor.

'Parachutes! We make parachutes,' blurted out Rayon. 'I once saw The Josh tie a handkerchief to a soldier doll with strings and drop it out of a window. It almost broke its fall.'

'Oh, parachutes! Very good, Mr Stuntdustbunny,' said Knickers. 'Out of what shall we make parachutes then, dear Rayon?'

'Fuzzballs,' declared Twill. 'We each grab a bunch, hang on tight and jump. They're fluffy and airheaded, they'll slow us down. Look.'

Twill waved a thread towards the attic window, where a beam of sunshine poking through the murky attic skylight created a pillar of light. Fuzzballs, having been launched by the laundry cycle, were still dancing and frolicking in the tiny draughts and micro-convection currents, catching the light and glowing with glee.

'I like it. Cruel, yet effective,' said Knickers. 'Isn't he clever, that Twill?' she went on to Rayon. 'That idea about parachutes – genius.'

Rayon had just enough time to say *'But I...'* before Twill pointed out that the laundry cycle had stopped. In the silence, Rayon, Knickers, Twill and Stour rolled themselves over to the edge of the dark chasm they'd popped out of and peered down into the darkness. The fuzzballs gathered close around them, taking turns to peer over the edge and ask each other 'Go whee?'

'Time to go,' ordered Twill. 'Tether up as many fuzzballs as you can – and don't mind their squealing when you squeeze them tight.'

Twill, Stour, Rayon and Knickers rolled about, plucking up threadfuls of fuzzballs, clutching them like huge bouquets of balloons. Suitably tooled up, the dust bunnies and their unwilling whiny helpers made their way to the leaping-off point. Lined up at the edge of the gap between the bricks, Rayon decided this didn't seem like such a good idea after all.

'Just one thing,' asked Rayon. 'How do we know when to stop?'

'Oh, you'll know,' replied Stour. 'Anyway, you're not made out of glass, you won't break.'

'Everyone ready?' asked Twill. Before he had time to say 'no', Rayon watched Twill, Stour and Knickers roll over the edge and disappear under an umbrella of fuzzballs, into the blackness.

All of a sudden, being left alone was worse than the thought of a big fall in the dark, so Rayon jumped too.

Any light seeping down from the attic above rapidly faded into darkness as he fell. How fast, he couldn't tell. Couldn't be that fast, he reasoned, as his threads weren't flapping. Rayon's parachute fuzzballs stopped their complaining about being nipped into a bunch and they, and Rayon, fell silent as they sank into the darkness between the walls, any sense of movement or time fading.

Maybe I'm not falling anymore, thought Rayon. *Maybe I've stopped and I just don't know it yet.*

After a period of time, when nothing changed at all – it may have been very long or perhaps longer – Knickers' voice floated up from somewhere below.

'Can you see that light?' she called out, but it wasn't Rayon she was talking to.

'Yes. And it's getting brighter,' came Twill's reply. Rayon felt a wave of relief sweep over him. Contact with the real world was re-established.

'That's outside light,' shouted Stour from below.

'How can you tell?' shouted back a doubtful Knickers.

'The photons are fresher.'

Even though he couldn't see Knickers, Twill or Stour anywhere, Rayon could see a greyish pool of light below him.

Falling closer to the source, Rayon could see light from the outside spilling in around a white cable coming through a coarsely drilled hole. The cable passed through the gap between the walls and went into the house, through another poorly finished hole in the inside wall.

When there was enough light to see properly, Rayon looked down on three canopies of fuzzballs, much closer than he expected. Rayon heard Twill shout out a warning.

'That's fresh air blowing in through that hole! Watch for sidewinds.'

Landing close to Twill, Stour and Knickers, Rayon bounced a couple of times before coming to a complete halt. They released their bouquets of fuzzballs, who shook themselves back into shape with some indignant humphing and cross looks, then everybunny went quiet as they took stock of where they were. Twill, Knickers, Stour, Rayon and attendant fuzzballs had landed on a dusty strip of ground, lit by thin slivers of outside light peeking in around the cable. Where the cable went into the house, a dim light leaked through the hole.

'Oh, that's what I like to see,' said Twill. 'Good, old-fashioned, apathetic workmanship,' and he directed their attention to where the cable went into the house.

'See!' exclaimed Stour. 'Access!'

'Holes!' squealed Rayon's fuzzballs, as they wriggled out of his grip and rolled off towards the brightest light. 'Let's play tunnels! First through wins.'

'Not that way, you fuzzwits,' shouted Rayon. 'That's outside. Other way.'

'Let's play tunnels! First through other way wins.'

'No, not this way either,' said Twill, stepping out in front of the tumbling fuzzballs so that they came to a halt in a soft, squishy pile in front of him.

'Rayon, will you get those fuzzballs under control? Stour, reconnoitre first and see if it's safe to proceed.'

'If it's not, can we send the fuzzballs in anyway?' asked Knickers.

'Yours first, then mine.'

'They're not mine,' protested Rayon as he waved multiple threads at his herd of fuzzballs. He was trying, not very successfully, to stop them rolling off into the darkness to play hide and... well, just hide.

'Yes, we are,' came gleeful fuzzball voices from the darkness.

With the fuzzballs distracted, Stour rolled alongside the cable until he came to where it passed through the inner wall and into the house. He had to wriggle and squirm a bit to squeeze into the cable hole to get a better look, but his sturdy fibres were woven for jobs like this and didn't break or snag. When Stour re-emerged, he reported they were behind the television stand, that no people seemed to be present, active or in couch potato mode, and that he deemed it safe to proceed.

Rayon, Knickers, Twill and Stour, with their entourage of fuzzballs in tow, squished up and wiggled their way through the poorly-executed drill hole, following the television cable and trying hard not to snag too many threads on the rough bits. They all clumped up at the exit hole, with Stour wriggling to the front to have what he called a '*shufti*', although Rayon thought it looked a lot like just looking around.

'Still all clear.'

They all squeezed through the hole to join Stour. A fat white cable lay ahead of them. It was level at first, not too far above the floor; but then it started curving upwards, very much upwards, higher and higher in a big, swooping curve. The highest point of the cable terminated at the peak of a lofty mound of fake wood shelves and boxy bits, presumably the lair of the screen and monitor dust bunnies.

'Right,' said Twill. 'Out, then up. In line, single file. Rayon first, fuzzballs next. Stour, you cover the rear. Go slowly on the steep bits, but there might be enough static to help us cling on a bit better.

Rayon, when you get to the top, look for a place where we can stop and re-group. Is that clear?'

'Eh, yes, I guess so,' agreed Rayon.

'Crystalline, sir,' snapped back Stour.

'Oh yes, I agree, too,' said Knickers. 'That is such a good idea. Very well thought out. Yes, I am all for your idea.' Then, nudging Rayon enthusiastically, she continued. 'Doesn't Twill have good ideas? And isn't he well-entangled?'

'Your electrons are wandering again,' muttered Stour to Knickers from safely behind Rayon.

All lined up as per orders, the dust bunnies and fuzzballs started to climb.

CHAPTER 7

The ascent up the cable, although slow, wasn't particularly arduous, but looking down gave Rayon the collywobbles. He didn't mind floating about in mid-air, but he discovered he didn't like standing above it. At the top, the cable got steep and every dust bunny had to climb up using lots of threads at a time. The fuzzballs couldn't get a proper grip and kept sliding back down on top of each other. Twill and Knickers lent a thread and shunted the last clump of fuzzballs up and over onto the flat area, where the cable connected to a black plastic box. Stour had to grab one fuzzball who was about to slide back down the cable again.

'Aww, please, just once,' whined the fuzzball.

'Oh yes, go on,' pleaded another.

'We could all slide together!'

'Wheee!' they all cried, making a run for the edge again.

'Oh no you don't, you wee scamps,' said Stour intercepting them just before they all tumbled off the top of the box. He bumped and herded them back together with Twill, Knickers and Rayon, well away from the edge. Although a bit dusty up here, there weren't any dust bunnies visible.

'These monitor and screen bunnies, made from invisible threads, are they?' asked Knickers after a while.

'They're probably just resting,' replied Twill. 'I've heard they're nocturnal. Or watching.'

'None of the screens are on. What can they be watching?' asked Knickers.

'Us,' replied Twill.

RAYON THE DUST BUNNY AND A VACUUM ABHORRED

That made everybunny look around warily.

'I heard they come out for afternoon TV,' added Stour. 'Anyway, they're sure to be here. There's no visible trace of recent cleaning – or any cleaning, come to that. Nice set-up they have here.'

'Welcome funambulists,' said a loud voice suddenly. 'Welcome to our humble abode.'

'Yaarg!' said Rayon, Twill, Stour and Knickers in reply, their threads and fibres springing out in all directions at once in alarm. They spun around to see a small, dense, grey dust bunny who had crept up behind them, his threads thrown wide in welcome.

'Welcome, I say again.'

'And hello to you. For the first time,' said Knickers, trying to gather her wayward threads back to some semblance of decency.

'You're our first visitors, you know,' said the grey dust bunny. 'We've never had visitors before.'

Crowds of equally small and dense dust bunnies were easing themselves out into the open from between the cooling slots of the television monitor. From in, under and around the cable box, more dust bunnies, all looking very much the same, trouped out to greet the visiting dust bunnies. The bickering started as soon as the welcoming committee of monitor and screen dust bunnies convened.

'They're spelunkers, too, you know, not just funambulists,' pointed out a dust bunny near the front. 'They came out of that hole.'

'They're not speleologists just because they crawled out of a hole in the wall,' said a dust bunny from the back of the pack.

'It's only speleology if they're sciencing,' replied the first dust bunny. 'What they did was just crawling, wriggling and falling somewhere dark. That's not an activity in and of itself.'

'It is too,' said the other dust bunny. 'It's called spelunking, you know. All that wriggling through uncomfortably dark, tight spaces.'

'Never mind that. Just say hello nicely and do the introductions.'

'Hello, I'm Rayon,' said Rayon as he rolled forward to interrupt the monitor dust bunnies, holding out a thread in greeting.

'Oh, thank goodness. That could've gone on forever,' said Twill quietly to Knickers. 'You ever meet a bookshelf dust bunny?'

'Only once,' she replied. 'I fell asleep when it started explaining… well, everything, really.'

'Well, I think this lot are cut from the same cloth.'

After a long discussion amongst themselves about titles, one monitor dust bunny, identical to all the others, was finally delegated as Temporary Plenopotentiary Without Portfolio because it was the longest title they could come up with in a hurry. He was given a shove and told to say hello and shake threads. The small spark coming from Rayon didn't appear to disturb it.

'Excuse me,' Rayon apologised.

'Not at all, young Rayon,' said the dust bunny. 'We've all done it and we're accustomed to the whiff of high voltages around here. I'm Doctor Crick.' He indicated the front row of monitor dust bunnies. 'And this is Einstein, Heinz Wolf, Doctor Spock, HAL 9000, Professors Cox, Al-Khalili, Du Sautoy and Higgs. This is Fermi, Dirac, Maxwell, Newton, Susskind, Faraday, Berners-Lee, Hawking, Sagan, Schrodinger, Darwin, Penrose and Oppenheimer.' The Doctor Crick dust bunny waved vaguely towards the rest of the dust bunnies peering out from gaps in the back of the television. 'The rest are just daytime television bunnies.'

'How do you do, all of you. Rayon. Of a hat,' said Rayon, waving a thread halfheartedly at them and worrying if he shouldn't have bowed instead.

'Don't you have proper names?' interrupted Stour.

'These are proper names,' sniffed a monitor dust bunny in the front row. 'Distinguished, famous names, I might add.'

'But not yours,' said Knickers, who was also curious now.

'We borrowed them.'

RAYON THE DUST BUNNY AND A VACUUM ABHORRED

'But why?' asked Twill. 'Our names are what we're made of. It's what dust bunnies do.'

After a silence and a big sigh, the dust bunny calling itself Oppenheimer explained.

'Not much goes on back here, you know. All we have are television programmes and the Internet. It's not a socially high-traffic area like the couch, with all manner of materials and fabrics coming and going. Back here, what fluff there is comes from what's around us, so if we did it your way we'd all be called Couch, Carpet or Curtain.'

'Oh, so you have nicknames?' said Stour.

'We prefer nom de guerre,' huffed a slightly put-out dust bunny next to Oppenheimer.

'Shouldn't that be noms de guerre?' asked another.

' I'd prefer nom de plume.'

'Nom, nom, nom,' added the fuzzballs.

'Pseudonyms, then. Will that do for everyone?' said Oppenheimer in a loud voice.

'So, as you say, not much goes on here,' said Twill.

'Not a great deal. We watch the pictures and listen to the words. On the television and the computer. That's about it. But we do learn a great deal.'

'Oh yes,' agreed a nearby dust bunny, 'a great deal of very useful information.'

And all the surrounding monitor dust bunnies nodded sagely in agreement.

'We especially like television with lots of facts and experiments and machines,' said Oppenheimer. 'With odd-looking scientists wandering about on mountain tops, explaining the universe and all the bits in it.'

'Oh yes, they're our favourites,' said a dust bunny with a Ph.D and two Nobel prizes.

'Oh, so you'll know all about entropy then,' piped up Knickers.

'Ah…' said one dust bunny after a extended silence that said more than words.

'Well…' added another.

'You see…' finished a third.

'No, we don't see, that's why we're asking you,' replied an increasingly frazzled Knickers. 'The central vac is going to be mended and there's going to be a tidying, a big tidying, even back here, I imagine. We're trying to stop it, but Yarn said not to worry because entropy was on our side.'

'So, there is a Yarn, then? In the attic?' asked Higgs, nudging up to the front.

'Yes, to both.'

'We saw Yarn, we saw the Yarn,' sang the fuzzballs. 'Dark as night he was with stars in, sparkling, sparkling, the big dark particle.'

Giggling at their own audacity, the fuzzballs tumbled away off to acquaint themselves with their new surroundings and hosts.

'Entropy?' prompted Knickers.

'It's the natural tendency of the universe to fall apart eventually,' answered a dust bunny by the name of Penrose. 'Everything around us, large and small, is falling apart, but at different speeds. Snowballs melt to water quicker than mountains turn to sand, but it all falls apart in the end, even stars and galaxies. Entropy's what happens when the universe stops tidying up.'

'Now, why would Yarn be pontificating about entropy?' wondered the dust bunny called itself Hawking.

'This blue one turned up. The Mum saw it,' explained Stour, waving a thread in Rayon's direction.

'Not "*it*",' corrected Rayon. 'His name is Rayon.'

'Sorry,' said Stour. 'Rayon here accidentally engendered a cleaning by being blindingly, startlingly, obviously very blue.'

Rayon started to splutter, but Knickers spoke up first.

RAYON THE DUST BUNNY AND A VACUUM ABHORRED

'I was there too, remember. It's not all Rayon's fault.'

Rayon was about to acknowledge Knicker's gracious defence, but she went on.

You can't blame Rayon. You have to blame whoever it was who mixed up that lurid and tasteless shade of blue; you need to whine at a colour-blind chemist.'

'Look, I think we're getting a bit off-topic here,' said Twill, rolling out in front of the assembled dust bunnies. 'Professors, this entropy, can it stop the central vac?'

'Hmmm,' hummed one in a very learned way.

'The second law of thermodynamics against the central vac?' pondered another.

'They have laws against central vacs? That sounds promising,' Knickers whispered to Rayon.

'Let us think about that.' The professors went into a grey huddle and conferred noisily. After another heated argument, Schrodinger was nominated and thrust out to deliver their carefully considered opinion.

'Well, in the long term, yes,' he said. 'Entropy will defeat the central vac. The heating and cooling cycles will take their toll on the lighter plastics so they will embrittle and crack, then fracture and break off into small pieces. Other plastics like insulation will slowly dry up and crack, metal contacts will be prone to heat stress, pitting, corrosion and wear. Any dampness in the air will encourage rust and vibrations should encourage it to shake itself to pieces eventually. Or the bearings in the motor will lose their lubrication and run red hot so they seize up solid, welded to itself.'

An appreciative '*ooooh*' came from the highly attentive fuzzballs and an engrossed Stour.

Schrodinger went on. 'Additionally, the seals and gaskets keeping The Wind in the central vac will shrivel and crack, causing loss of suction. Vibration will further loosen bits here and there, switches will lose their on and off click. Finally, it'll be hauled off to the dump or melted down as scrap metal. Later, the sun will expand and burn the earth and the remains of the central vac into space, where its very atoms will be dispersed into an ever-expanding universe, perhaps to be synthesised by the power of a supernova back into new elements.'

'And could all this happen before, say, next week?' asked Knickers.

The monitor bunnies went into another muttering huddle. After a patience-straining age, Schrodinger came back with an answer.

'In our carefully considered opinion, after weighing all the options, we have a consensus on that issue.'

'Did he just answer or sneeze?' whispered Stour to Knickers.

'Shhh. Which is?' asked Knickers.

'No.'

'Oh. So, this entropy isn't much use then?' said Knickers. 'We're all going to get tidied up next week.'

'Well, there is another possibility,' said Schrodinger. Not a good one, though.'

Twill prompted him this time, wishing he had a pointy stick to hurry him along. 'Which is?'

'Fire.'

'What's wrong with a burning central vac?' asked a puzzled Stour. Knickers' shrug suggested she couldn't see what the problem was either.

'Could burn the house down,' pointed out Rayon.

'Ah, yes. That,' said Knickers as the penny dropped. Stour's still quizzical look, however, hinted that his penny was still somewhere in mid-flight.

'You!' snapped Schrodinger, pointing at Stour with a rigid thread and stern gaze. 'What do you suppose burns first when a central vac catches fire?'

'Bits of central vac, I would imagine.'

'No, not bits of central vac. Bits of dust bunnies.'

Stour's penny landed, but his brief, bright dawn of understanding was suddenly dimmed by the dark, looming clouds of the implications.

'Oh, that's not good.'

It went very quiet around the back of the television.

'Consider,' said Schrodinger as he rolled up and down with his threads clasped behind him. 'With time and infrequent maintenance, dust bunnies, drawn in to the central vac by cooling fans or spinning rotors, will clump up in what cramped, low, airflow niches they can find in and around the electric motor. But, while the dust bunnies have been enclumpulating over the years, the electromechanical parts of the motor have become pitted, dirty and inefficient.'

Schrodinger looked around, pausing to make sure he had everyone's attention. 'Eventually, called on to power the central vac, the electricity struggles to flow freely. Sparks fly instead. One lands on the dust bunnies nearby. At first there's only singeing, smouldering and smoke. But the spinning motor fans the tiny glowing embers into life, increasing the rate of combustion and soon there are flames and no escape. First to be eaten by fire are the dust bunnies closest to the electrical contacts. Then, flames reach out to consume other clumps of dust bunnies, spreading the fire into the interior of the central vac until the wires themselves burn, buckle and twist and the burning plastics make thick, black smoke and the whole unit deforms and comes screaming to a final, fiery halt. Then, as you correctly pointed out earlier,' said Schrodinger waving a thread at Rayon, 'the house burns down, taking everything with it.'

There was a solemn silence as all the dust bunnies present dwelt upon the horror of it all. The fuzzballs, meanwhile, had found a cooling fan and were pushing each other into it to see how far out the other end they would fly. Twill broke the silence.

'How likely is that to happen? The fiery death option?'

'Not impossible, but incredibly unlikely,' conceded Schrodinger.

'So why's the central vac dead this time if it isn't entropy?' asked Rayon.

'Choked on toothpicks and wet paper towels from the kitchen is what we heard,' chimed in the Professor Cox dust bunny.

'Not a nozzleful of entropy then?' said Knickers.

'There might have been potato peelings, too.'

'Perhaps somebunny in the kitchen could help us?' suggested Rayon.

'Right! Next objective: the kitchen,' said Twill.

'That Twill,' said Knickers, nudging Rayon in the side threads. 'Doesn't he have good ideas?'

Any further conversation was curtailed when The Josh and The Andrew came into the room, slumped onto the couch, assumed the couch potato position and turned on the television. The Mum and The Dad joined them. Behind the television, Rayon could feel the sudden surge of electricity, making his threads tingle.

'Oh no you don't,' said an observant and wary Knickers, moving a safe distance away from Rayon's wayward threads. The fuzzballs plumped up alarmingly, too, and they bounced off each other like colliding beach balls. The light from the television flashed and abruptly changed colours – sometimes, Rayon noted, in relation to the booming and crashing noises. The roaring and explosions stopped and then there was some music. This was followed by someone singing about softness and cleanliness where it matters and then abruptly it went quiet.

'What just happened?' whispered Rayon.

'Commercial break,' explained Knickers.

'I'm sorry,' said Rayon, puzzled. 'What broke?'

'It's a thing that happens on the television,' explained Knickers. 'Something interrupts what they're looking at. They say the bad

RAYON THE DUST BUNNY AND A VACUUM ABHORRED

words, shout "*mute*" and it goes quiet for a while.'

'So what do we do now?'

'Oh, they'll be televisioning for hours now, we're safe enough here,' said Knickers.

'We'll stay here until the next bright, then make our way to the kitchen,' said Twill. 'The kitchen dust bunnies seem to have more practical solutions than this lot, however dense their threads. Stour, tell those fuzzballs they're staying here and not to wander off.'

Stour rolled over to the fuzzballs and explained very explicitly what he personally would do to them, thread by thread, should they wander out of sight. Somewhat cowed, the still-lightly-zapped fuzzballs bunched up as best they could in a safe corner and muttered dark things to each other. Dark obviously soon turned to rude, because the whole pile of fuzzballs started to quake and barely-suppressed squawks and giggling could be heard from within.

'I saw a television commercial for a vacuum cleaner once,' announced Stour in an oddly loud voice and with an obvious glare at the pile of fuzzballs. 'Some dreadful person had harnessed The Wind in tornado form in a grotesque see-through cylinder. You could see all kinds of tribes of dust bunnies and fuzzballs being sucked up and trapped in there, hurtling around and around, pressed up hard against the insides, totally squished until the bits were sucked down into the parts of the machine they don't show you, never to be seen or heard of ever again. Especially never heard of.'

The chastened fuzzballs were silenced and fell into a sulking heap. However, the quiet was soon chased away by the television being un-muted and the big voices starting again. The monitor and screen dust bunnies settled down into their nooks and crannies, making themselves comfortable for what was obviously going to be a long time.

'Oh good, a sciencey documentary series,' said one of the professor monitor dust bunnies to Rayon. 'That's what we like best.'

'I do hope they put a physicist up a mountain,' explained another excitable screen dust bunny to Knickers.

'Who could ask for anything more?'

When televisioning was over for the day, the people fled for the exits. The Josh was sent back home, The Mum and The Andrew went upstairs, leaving The Dad to switch everything electrical off.

The Dad turned off the last light in the room and, making his way out, walked into a chair and said the bad words before limping off upstairs. In the dark above, around and under the television and its peripherals, the warmth remained long into the night and the dust bunnies rested.

RAYON THE DUST BUNNY AND A VACUUM ABHORRED

CHAPTER 8

Night-time fell all around the house. Downstairs, the last of the heat from the television and computer screens ticked away into silence, the television and screen bunnies snug under their blanket of electronic warmth. In between the circuit boards and shiny boxes and colourful cables, the computer dust bunnies shuffled about a bit to make room for the extra bits of fluff brought in by people movements, convection and cooling fans.

In the lounge, dust bunnies sank further down between the cushions of the couch and, behind all the good bits of furniture that don't get moved about often, long-established colonies of dust bunnies settled into their respective niches, nooks, channels, gullies, crevasses, hollows and hidey-holes.

In the kitchen, the dust bunnies under the fridge, the dust bunnies behind the stove and the dust bunnies along the tops of the wall cabinets had all clumped up snug for the night, secure in the knowledge that the zeal necessary for a kitchen clean was usually the first thing people ran out of. The fuzzballs in the laundry had finally run out of puff and settled into drifts, hummocks and mounds. It was dark down there anyway, so there was nowhere to play.

Upstairs, however, in the spare room, things were stirring.

'Will you lot hurry up?'

'I've lost my favourite red thread somewhere,' wailed a biddy from under the bed.

'You'll lose all your threads if you don't hurry up,' urged another voice from the shadows. 'The central vac won't wait for you to find your precious red threads. Come on, puff and clump up, puff and clump up.'

The dust bunnies were fleeing the haven of the spare room en masse. The news of the tidy up brought by the fuzzball was bad enough, but there was more. News of The Mum's forthcoming baby had prompted a phone call to her sister, The Vera. Then, The Mum had words with The Dad and tomorrow, it was agreed, everything in the spare room was going to be turned upside down and inside out in preparation for The Vera's visit.

All those nice stacks of cardboard boxes with their flaps and crannies, well out of the way of The Wind, ventilation or passing people, were to be moved into the basement. The bed was to be excavated of all clothing, no matter how many layers deep, and that meant tribes of displaced dust bunnies searching for somewhere safe to settle when the tidying was over. In the absence of a functional central vac, there was going to be cleaning of the floor in the spare room using the old rolling wheezing, whining dinosaur of a vacuum cleaner, the one kept at the back of the cupboard, where many a dust bunny languished in ironic smugness.

A room-scale dust bunny migration is a majestic event. The sheer number and volume of dust bunnies on the move would present an irresistible and deeply gratifying target for an enthusiastic tidy-upper, a slow-motion avalanche of soft focus and fluff, many a bellyful for a busy central vac. So migrations only ever happen at night when no-one's watching. Dust bunnies clump together loosely in long rolls, or in rough attempts at spheres, because they roll faster and further across a wooden floor like that. In between the densest clumps of rolling, bobbing dust bunnies lay a drifting soft, grey fog; misty fuzzballs mostly, still unfettered by the threads of experience.

Clutching on tight to each other in a mix of nervousness and excitement, the fuzzballs rolled in rippling soft, silvery grey waves, away from the spare room, borne forward by a breeze not much more than a sigh.

RAYON THE DUST BUNNY AND A VACUUM ABHORRED

Progress was stately and steady. Elder dust bunnies remained at the rear, keeping the lighter accumulations from getting too distracted by the novelty of being out so late at night and rolling off on their own. The larger tribes from under the bed, wardrobe or desk clumped more densely and rolled more sedately. With a tendency to clump with their own, clutches, drifts and wispy clans of dust bunnies of denim, cotton, pyjama, underwear and sock as yet unaffiliated to a tribe, rolled, bounced and tumbled across the floor at slightly varying speeds – especially the lightbulb bunnies, who almost danced along in the moonlight as the sleeping house breathed slow and deep.

With the moon peeking in through the spare room window to see what all the activity was about, she shone a cool, silver light over the last great waves of those dust bunnies from far, far under the bed making their slow, majestic exit from the spare bedroom. Past The Andrew's room they went and across the floor towards the stairs, tumbling between the railings and flowing down the stairs in a cataract of hope.

By dawn, the spare room, despite the evacuation, was still not quite barren. Older, bolder perimeter dust bunnies of a rougher weave, who had seen this kind of thing before, just snuggled back deeper into the trench that ran around the room where the carpet met the wall. They knew that the wheezing old beater of a vacuum cleaner had neither the puff nor the brushes to reach back this far.

As long as they held on tight with their robust fibres, they'd still be in their sanctuary of stillness after the prehistoric vacuum cleaner had done its feeble worst and was wheeled back into its cave.

As the day grew lighter, it revealed the crowding downstairs. Thick clods of refugee dust bunnies from the spare room were still struggling to find somewhere dark, unregarded and, above all, turbulence-free. All the good spots were taken, especially in the cupboard under the stairs, where clouds of dust bunnies were now spilling out from under all the shoes. Great tufts of displaced dust bunnies were sitting there in plain sight, near the hinges, with no place left to go.

Most of the downstairs rooms were already well-populated with long-established colonies. The downstairs dust bunnies resented the intrusion of mere clothing fibres into what they saw as their superior realm, *'showcasing the best quality upholstery, drapery and carpetry fibres in the house'*. Then, a dust bunny from upstairs said that *'carpetry'* wasn't a word and to shimmy over anyways because 'We're all in this together, no matter what we're woven from.'

The newly assembled ranks of dust bunnies in the downstairs rooms allowed themselves some cautious optimism when the heating came on. Heating jostled the molecules, created convection currents, stirring the air and dispersing more of the lighter-fibred dust bunnies into quiet pools of still air in the lee of corners and edges, or hoisting them up to settle somewhere good in the upper reaches, above the eyeline, on picture frames, light shades and curtains. Soon, the people would start moving about, too, stirring up the air and dissipating the remaining shoals of unanchored dust bunnies more evenly, presenting less of an amassed affront to The Mum's sense of domestic order.

The Mum, awake and functional first, thumped down the stairs, the trailing edge of her flowing pink gown gently gathering up the last of the spare room sluggards and dust bunnies-come-lately who had been caught out on the stairs. Caught on her hems, the last of these spare room dust bunnies were whisked downstairs with limousine smoothness into the kitchen where, after a quick about-turn from The Mum, they were ejected from her hems towards the safety of the food pantry. Here, kitchen dust bunnies, with more than a hint of cardboard to them, hustled the slightly astonished newcomers from upstairs safely back into the unvisited recesses where the lentils were kept.

RAYON THE DUST BUNNY AND A VACUUM ABHORRED

The Dad descended too quickly to pick up passengers; he was already late for work.

Under strict instructions from The Mum in the kitchen, relayed upstairs by The Dad to get up and get down here, The Andrew huffed and stomped down the stairs last, his flapping pyjama legs wafting a clutch or two of miscellaneous dust bunnies at the bottom of the stairs into the room where the television was. A few more were carried in his wake into the kitchen, where the under-the-fridge dust bunnies made space to squeeze them in.

Some displaced dust bunnies were lucky enough to be swept into drifts far under the stairs when The Dad was flapping umbrellas, shoes and scarves about looking for the car keys that were quite clearly on the shelf behind him. After a moment of exasperation and another of illumination when The Dad turned around to see his keys right in front of him, he yelled a farewell, opened the front door and let The Wind in. Those dust bunnies from upstairs who hadn't found a safe place to anchor for the day (and there were still drifts and banks of them still in plain sight), were lofted off the floor and sent spinning and spiralling all around the downstairs rooms, until The Dad closed the door behind him and The Wind stopped as suddenly as it came.

With The Wind gone, the airborne dust bunnies gently settled into the low pressure havens and onto all the available surfaces and edges, much to the discombobulation and dismay of the indigenous dust bunnies, who didn't like the unwanted visitors sitting on their heads.

Fed and watered, The Andrew was told by The Mum to go back upstairs, get dressed and de-pigsty his room.

'The central vac gets repaired tomorrow,' she said, 'so get everything off the floor, even under the bed. In fact, especially under the bed. Aunt Vera is coming later today and your dad is going to tidy the spare room, so don't make a mess.'

The Andrew yelled something back from the top of the stairs that may or may not have been language, withdrew into his room and set about excavating his debris.

Plodding from the kitchen with her morning coffee into the television room and swirling more wispy grey banks of dust bunnies in with her hems, the groaning Mum flopped gratefully into the couch. She heaved her feet and swollen ankles up onto the footrest and turned the television on.

Around the back of the television, Knickers was the second dust bunny to notice the television had been turned on because she woke up to a fully-electrified Rayon. Once again, he was clinging to her with every highly-charged fibre of his being.

'Ahh!' she cried and tried to flap Rayon off her. 'Get off, get off.'

But she couldn't escape his electrostatic grasp or his endless apologising.

'I'm sorry, I'm sorry, I am so sorry,' said Rayon as he tried to peel his disobliging threads away from Knickers.

'Well, that makes two of us,' replied Knickers as she gave up struggling. By now, the fuzzballs had woken up, too, and were asking awkward questions.

'What you doing?'

'Why are you rubbing your threads together?'

'Are you rubbing threads because you like each other?'

'No, no, no,' came the short-tempered answer from Knickers. 'This is an accident. Now, stop being mostly useless empty space and peel us apart.'

After some pathetic tugging from the clusters of fuzzballs, Twill and Stour came to her rescue and, one by one, prised her threads from Rayon's.

'Come on, you two,' said Twill. 'This is no time for romance. We've got company.'

'Aye,' said Stour. 'Lots of company. Moved in last night. Look at this.'

RAYON THE DUST BUNNY AND A VACUUM ABHORRED

Stour led them to the edge of a television box to peer over the edge. Directly in front of them, on the couch, sprawled The Mum, in pink – and floods of it. Stour directed their attention to the floor. Around the edges of television room was a rising grey mist of displaced dust bunnies embanking at the walls and rounding off the corners of the room, where dust bunnies clamoured in vain to get away from the open spaces. More wads of dust bunnies had settled under the overhangs of every piece of furniture – under the couch, the comfy chairs, the uncomfy chairs, footstools, light-stands, magazine racks, CD stand, including that ugly old travel chest The Dad had thought so cool when he was at college. No niche, crevice, dent or fissure was left dust bunniless. Even between the cushions, under the The Mum herself, lay thickly-packed rolls of accumulated dust bunnies, unable to obscure or camouflage themselves in any fashion or form. Surely they'd be the first to go?

Drifts of the lighter dust bunnies had settled on every horizontal edge of every picture and mirror that hung on the walls, giving their edges a slightly out-of-focus look. The curtains had pyramids of dust bunnies tottering atop their skinny ridges. A clump of dust bunnies at the peak would waver, then tumble off the ridgeline to fall and add to the already deep heaps of denser dust bunnies that lay at the base of the curtains.

Gazing around the room from the vantage point of the television, Twill, Stour, Knickers and Rayon saw dust bunnies colonising every edge and every recess as densely as gannets on a cliff face (but very much quieter and smelling much less of fish).

'Oh,' said Knickers.

'That's what I thought,' said Stour. 'I've never seen such a mess.'

'Magnificent, but terrifying,' said Twill.

'Why "terrifying"?' asked Rayon. 'Isn't lots of dust bunnies a Good Thing?'

'In different circumstances, I'd say yes,' replied Twill. 'Today? No.

This presents a target-rich environment for a hostile tidy up.'

'How long do you suppose it would take for the central vac to, you know...' asked Rayon.

'Oh, oh, oh, stop,' interrupted Knickers. 'That's horrible, stop it. No more tidy talk. We have to do something.'

'Yarn said we shouldn't do anything,' pointed out Rayon. 'He said dust will prevail.'

'Well, it's certainly prevailing in here,' said Stour.

'Yes, but for how long?' replied Twill. 'The repairman comes on the next bright so we need to find out exactly what killed the central vac and see if we can't keep it dead.'

'That Professor Cox said the central vac died in the kitchen last time. We should ask there,' said Knickers.

The Mum stirred. Rising with majestic slowness, she extricated herself from the couch, turned the television off and, being the only one in the house with a sense of domestic order, put the remote control back on top of the television-related boxes. In doing so, her pink fluffy sleeve plucked up Rayon, Twill, Stour and Knickers and flipped the fuzzballs to the floor. As The Mum started her stately voyage back to the kitchen, the entourage of fuzzballs were swept up in her wake and bobbed along in tow, some of them hitching a lift on the trailing hem of her dressing gown, waving as they went. From their elevated position on The Mum's cuff, Rayon, Twill, Stour and Knickers looked down and saw thickets of mute, staring dust bunnies of all stripes, patterns and fabrics lining the floors, watching The Mum pass with fear and trepidation.

In the kitchen, Rayon, Twill, Stour and Knickers were cast off from The Mum's sleeve as The Mum opened the fridge door and stared into it, humming to herself. They floated down to the floor. Waiting for them, the relentlessly loyal fuzzballs had assembled and were bobbing up and down impatiently.

'What do we do now? What do we do now?' they wanted to know.

RAYON THE DUST BUNNY AND A VACUUM ABHORRED

'You be quiet, is what you do,' hissed Knickers after she landed. 'Now hush.'

The Mum finished plundering the fridge, closed the door and wandered off, too slowly to stir the air. Knickers rolled closer to the fridge and called out.

'Dust bunnies under the fridge. Room for four?'

CHAPTER 9

From under the fridge, dark shapes rolled cautiously into the light. At first glance, the dust bunnies de cuisine were the dirtiest dust bunnies Rayon had ever seen; not only were they almost as black as Yarn in density, but they were covered in bits, crumbs, shards, fragments and particles of all kinds of food. However, Rayon noticed that some of the fridge dust bunnies were free of food particles and had, instead, a fine gloss to their threads, giving them a lustrous smoothness. It was one of these well-groomed white linen dust bunnies who rolled out to greet them.

'Why, if it isn't Mademoiselle Knickers herself,' said the dust bunny, taking one of Knickers' threads in his and kissing it. 'May I say how delighted we are to have you with us again. I see you have brought guests.'

Turning to Rayon, Twill and Stour, he gave a gracious bow.

'Serviette, you old charmer you,' said Knickers. 'This is Rayon, Twill and Stour. Rayon, Twill and Stour, Serviette.'

Suddenly feeling rather primitive, they grunted hello and waved a bit of thread in his general direction.

'Enchanté,' he replied. 'Any friend of Mademoiselle Knickers is more than welcome here.' Serviette then ushered them with a graceful sweep of his threads to safety under the fridge. 'Come, come, let us find you somewhere more discreet and comfortable and then we can talk. M'sieur Rayon, I'm afraid you'll have to leave your fuzzballs at the door.'

'They're not my fuzzballs,' replied Rayon. 'They're with... well, all of us.'

RAYON THE DUST BUNNY AND A VACUUM ABHORRED

'Nevertheless...' insisted Serviette.

Stour came to the rescue by corralling all the fuzzballs into a heap, threatening them with recycling if they so much as moved a thread until they got back. Cowed by his stern voice and the strangeness of their circumstances, the fuzzballs rolled into a pile and glowered at Stour. But they did stay put.

With a nod of thanks to Stour, Serviette led them onwards.

'He's a bit smooth, isn't he?' whispered Rayon to Stour as Serviette ushered them all under the fridge.

' It's the olive oil,' replied Stour.

'But how does he stay so tidy?'

'Good grooming,' said Stour, trying unsuccessfully to flatten down and tidy up some of his more wayward threads. 'Never did get the hang of it.'

'Come, come. What we can we get for you?' asked Serviette as he rolled ahead of them. 'Perhaps some Parmesan crumbs? Bread, of course. Bits of dried herbs are over here at the sides. Watch for those bits of eggshell...'

'Serviette,' interrupted Kickers. 'We're not here for morsels, however delicious. There's trouble. The Mum's going to get the central vac mended. And soon.'

Serviette stopped and turned to Knickers. 'Non. You cannot be serious.'

'Very serious,' she replied. 'There's going to be a tidying.'

'Next bright,' confirmed Twill.

The joie de vivre leaked out of Serviette in one big sigh.

'I thought we had seen the last of that monster,' he said. 'So many of our brave dishcloth dust bunnies...' Serviette's voice trailed away into silence.

Rayon knew he was missing something here, but he also knew this wasn't the time to ask. It was Twill who broke the silence.

'Monsieur Serviette,' he said gently. 'Our condolences. But

please, we have to ask. How did your dishcloth dust bunnies kill the central vac? Even Yarn couldn't give us any advice.'

Serviette looked up. 'You went to see Le Yarn?'

'Aye,' piped up Stour. 'But he told us to do nothing.'

'Perhaps that would have been good advice,' replied Serviette sadly. 'It has become remarkably crowded in these parts recently.'

'You killed the central vac?' asked an impressed Rayon.

'Yes, we, le mouton de cuisine. We clogged it,' said Serviette, his spirits rising at the memory. 'They made the ultimate sacrifice. They, the dishcloth dust bunnies as you call them. Last week, when the central vac was unleashed, it swallowed a broken toothpick covered in food and it stuck in its guts behind the walls. Then, it snapped up a clump of our dishcloth dust bunnies but they were still damp, so they snagged on the toothpick. Then, anytime a dust bunny was consumed, those gallant and brave dishcloth dust bunnies snatched them up and held them tight, creating a dense mass that choked the central vac. We could hear it whining, even right at the back of the fridge, where we had all fled for safety.'

'Then what happened?' asked a rapt Rayon.

'Nothing could pass the dishcloth dust bunnies' blockade, no matter how hard the central vac inhaled,' replied Serviette. 'Soon, it couldn't even pick up a paper napkin fluff, so The Dad pulled its tail out and put the central vac back into its foul pit. We only heard its awful screeching start again upstairs yesterday. What happened? Has it escaped?'

'The Mum invoked a cleaning because she caught sight of Rayon and Knickers here canoodling out on the open floor,' said Stour. 'Ouch!' he added after a scowling Knickers pinged him with an elastic.

Serviette rolled back a bit and looked at Knickers in a way that made her feel quite uncomfortable.

'We were not canoodling,' she explained most emphatically.

RAYON THE DUST BUNNY AND A VACUUM ABHORRED

'I do not care if you canoodled or not,' replied Serviette. 'There is a time and a place for canoodling. I am just surprised that you, of all dust bunnies, were caught out in the open.'

'That's my fault, not hers,' said Rayon to Serviette. 'I'd just been newly entangled and we got into an electrostatic clinch.'

'And I couldn't pull myself away,' added Knickers.

'She's very attractive, you know,' said Rayon.

'Enough!' said Twill loudly and everybunny stopped talking to look at him. 'Serviette. The central vac. Is it dead or not?'

'Now, I'm not so sure,' replied Serviette. 'We could hear the dishcloth dust bunnies from where they snagged on the toothpick. They weren't stuck in the vile, corrugated throat of the central vac, le accordion du mort, but in its guts, behind the walls, where they say the tubes are smooth. I assume they are still there, but we have heard nothing more.'

'Can't they get out?' asked a horrified Rayon.

'They can go neither forward nor back,' replied Serviette. 'Not until the central vac is repaired. Then their destination is assured, I'm afraid.'

'The repairman is coming after next bright,' Twill reminded Serviette.

'You are certain?' asked a worried Serviette. 'Then come, come, there is no time to lose. We must tell the kitchen dust bunnies to scatter and save themselves.' He started rolling towards the cooker.

'No, wait, there's nowhere to go,' interrupted Twill, snagging a thread onto Serviette to hold him back. 'All the good spots are gone. The Dad's cleaning the spare room today. All the spare room dust bunnies migrated last dark. There's displacement all over the house.'

'Really?' replied Serviette. 'I did not know it was quite so serious. But we still have to tell the rest to secure themselves as best they can. We cannot leave them in the dark.'

Would have thought that was the best place to be, thought Rayon, but kept it to himself.

'Serviette's right,' said Twill. 'We need to warn as many kitchen dust bunnies as we can. Spread out – you take that side of the kitchen, we'll take this side. We'll meet in the gap beside the sink.'

'Oh, merci, Monsieur Twill,' said Serviette. 'I will warn my compatriots under the fridge and in the pantry.' He turned to Knickers. 'Mademoiselle,' he said solemnly, 'it is my great misfortune to be entangled at a time when we may not meet again. Should that be the case, may I say it has been my great pleasure and lasting delight to have made your acquaintance.'

Serviette took a thread of Knickers' and pressed it affectionately between two of his. Then he released her and rolled back into the darkness under the fridge.

Then The Mum came in with her coffee cup and put it in the sink. Before she went back upstairs, she opened the kitchen door to take a stroll up the garden path and to let that nice, fresh, warm spring air blow the winter staleness away.

RAYON THE DUST BUNNY AND A VACUUM ABHORRED

CHAPTER 10

The perimeter dust bunnies in the spare room were right: The Dad was a reluctant and unenthusiastic cleaner. At floor level, the entrenched dust bunnies peered over the lip of the carpet to watch The Dad shunt a roaring, worn-out, upright vacuum cleaner towards them. For all its noise and fury, the old vacuum cleaner didn't have any puff left and its frayed and time-softened bristles could do little more than spank the carpet gently rather than dislodge stubborn particles of dirt and tenacious dust bunnies.

Even when the roaring bulk of the cleaner was rolled right up against the walls, practically on top of them, the perimeter dust bunnies felt barely a tug on their fibres, so feeble was the breeze under the vacuum cleaner.

Much to the delight of the spare room dust bunnies, who had spurned the mass migration and stayed put, The Dad wasn't a terribly clever tidy-upper. They couldn't believe their good fortune – after stirring up the dust and dander with the cloddish vacuum cleaner, The Dad was now going to dust! And he wasn't using a fluffy duster, with its evil electrostatic grip, but a tired and tatty bit of cloth. And no whiffs of lemon-fresh polish, either.

The Dad flapped the soft cloth across the top of the picture frames and table light, flopped it about over the dressing-table and mirror and gave it a pointless wiggle in the general direction of the bedside table. Dislodged dust flew everywhere, unnoticed by The Dad. The little cirrus clouds of undifferentiated fluff that The Dad launched from the horizontal surfaces dispersed into light strata, collided with the wall, then drifted down ever so slowly to the floor, bulking up the perimeter dust bunnies nicely.

When The Dad made up The Vera's bed, two tribes of polycotton dust bunnies and one of pillow dust bunny were launched high into the air when he threw the sheets over the bed and started tucking them in. A woolly blanket yielded up stout and sturdy wool dust bunnies, while The Dad's further guddling about in the closet liberated a clutch of new dust bunnies, not quite certain of their own identity yet.

Even as The Dad was hustling the vacuum cleaner out of the spare room, tripping on cords and bumping the door frame, the newcomers were already being ushered by the more experienced perimeter dust bunnies to places of safety and comforting obscurity. By the time he called out that the spare room was done, the dust bunny count per square inch in The Vera's room was higher than when he'd started.

RAYON THE DUST BUNNY AND A VACUUM ABHORRED

CHAPTER 11

A dust bunny's relationship with The Wind is an ambivalent one. On one thread, The Wind, in its more benign moods, stirs the air gently, delivering dust bunnies around the house, getting them approximately and eventually to where they want or need to be. The Wind, with a little helping of turbulence from the passing inhabitants, is mainly responsible for maintaining the wide and even distribution of dust bunnies around the average family home.

On the other thread, The Wind is sometimes nothing but a big bully, blasting in through an open door, bludgeoning a dust bunny up, down, sideways, hither and yon, then out the door in the blink

When The Mum opened the door this time, a thuggish lump of air gate-crashed into the kitchen, rustling the curtains, bouncing off the walls and generally making itself unwelcome. Rayon, Knickers, Twill and Stour were slammed up hard against the side of a cupboard and pressed almost flat. Most of the cooker dust bunnies were safe, way back under the cooker itself; nevertheless, The Wind snatched up a clutch of those cooker dust bunnies that always loiter under the drawer where people keep their baking trays. Before they knew it, a few score of these sturdy dust bunnies were scooped up and whisked away out the open kitchen door, their fate now entirely dependent on weather conditions.

The dust bunnies at floor level weren't the only ones sent base over apex by the invading Wind. On top of the kitchen cupboards, there was a lost continent of undiscovered and undisturbed dust bunnies. Patches and drifts of them were snatched up by The Wind's blunt fists, bumped a few times, hard, off the ceiling, thus dislodging several threads, and then cast down to the floor, leaving them flimsy and feeble-minded.

As the air pressure equalised around the house, The Wind's obstreperous enthusiasm and energy rapidly diminished and a tense, wary mood settled on the dust bunnies.

Stour and Rayon reflated themselves, shook off some bits of dry cracker and tucked in a few threads that were in danger of becoming disentangled. Over by the fridge, Twill and Knickers dragged themselves out from under a mat of cupboard top dust bunnies who, being suddenly rendered lightweight, were now having a difficult time telling which way was up.

With the big gust gone, but the kitchen door still wide open, it was hard to tell what kind of mood The Wind was in now. A dust bunny could never tell if The Wind was going to suddenly get boisterous again. As a result, Stour was particularly careful to grapple on tight to the cooker before tentatively peering around the corner. He could see The Mum outside, up the garden path, basking in the sun, enjoying the first warm rays of a springtime sun. As he rolled out a bit further, all Stour could feel were the fading zephyrs and the feathery caress of slowly decaying vortices.

'Big Gus has gone now,' Rayon heard Stour call back to him.

Fast Eddy and Big Gus, thought Rayon. *Who are these people? I didn't know they lived here, too.* He rolled forward to take a look out the door. No sign of Gus or Eddy. But it did look nice outside. Being of a hat – and a winter hat, at that – Rayon didn't see much in the way of good weather, so the combination of sunshine and warm, caressing light breezes coming through the open door was quite new to him. He wriggled his threads to let the pleasant breeze pass through him.

'Wouldn't it be nice to fly in this?' asked a blissed-out Rayon.

'Don't you be liking that,' warned Stour as he watched Rayon get a bit too rapturous. 'Don't trust it. Even a warm Wind can be treacherous. Look at that! That's exactly what I mean.'

Stour was pointing a thread towards the door. 'That bright patch, drifting in the door.'

Rayon could see it now. A soft, fuzzy point in mid-air. Then he saw another. And another.

'That's down,' said Stour. 'Airborne down. Flying seeds whipped up by the wind. Obviously been hibernating somewhere dry – the garage, I shouldn't wonder.'

Several downy seeds had drifted right into the kitchen and Rayon watched as the tufts of silvery threads parachuted slowly to the floor, graceful as night falling, landing lightly on the tip of their elegant dark payload of seed.

'Might be dandelion, might be thistledown,' continued Stour. 'Don't know, doesn't matter. Just you keep an eye on them, young Rayon, and don't let them get too close.'

Rayon watched as the last of the airborne seeds settled to the floor with balletic grace. Then a breeze from the garden sent the down tumbling across the open expanse of the kitchen floor towards the sink unit. As they rolled, the lightweight down wove themselves into a flimsy tangle.

'They look harmless enough,' said Rayon as he watched the airborne down tumble by.

'Ha!' Stour said. 'You can't trust flying things. I once had a very close call with a feather from a duvet. Watch. And don't let go. If we get a gust or fast eddy...'

Them again, thought Rayon, but then he saw how closely Stour was watching the down's slow manoeuvres. Rayon got the sense of a terrible threat. *From something so pretty?* he thought. *Surely not.*

The tangles of airborne seeds bumped gently into the base of the sink unit. Rayon watched as a simple-threaded, tea towel dust bunny rolled out to say hello. A few other curious young dust bunnies ventured out from other cracks and holdfasts to peer at the elegant but mute newcomers. Soon, there was quite a cluster of dust bunnies around the down, trying to get them to answer questions and excitedly chattering amongst themselves.

Then the front doorbell rang. The bell was obviously loud enough for The Mum to hear, despite the fact she'd wandered off up the garden path with the magnificent serenity of a pink iceberg. On hearing the chimes, The Mum launched herself towards the house with all the haste of an intercontinental ballistic blancmange, rocketry in pink. Swaying prodigiously from side to side, The Mum flounced through the kitchen at max revs to the front door. The Vera had arrived!

The passing Mum's turbulence and choppy wake swept those curious tea towel dust bunnies, so keen to find out more about the down, right into their slender welcoming arms, delightful at first, but then relentless. Try as they might, the dust bunnies couldn't shake off their silent embrace. The more a dust bunny wriggled, the more the down wrapped itself around it. Rayon could see several dust bunnies knotted and intertwined with various clumps of down.

The Mum threw open the front door to greet The Vera. As the door was thrown open, an opportunistic gust of Wind pushed its way in past The Vera and The Mum in their welcoming hug. Rayon and Stour felt the sudden increase in local air pressure and instinctively held on tighter. As the unimpeded Wind rushed from front door to back, it snatched up the unmoored and weightless clumps of down and, with them, the entrapped dust bunnies.

Rayon watched the tea towel dust bunnies, borne aloft by the down, wriggle as they tried to escape, but it was no good. The clumps of dandelion and thistledown seeds carried them off on the arms of The Wind, through the door and outside.

'What happens to them now?' Rayon could still pick out the bright motes of down and dust bunny glowing brightly in the sunlight, dancing energetically in the outdoor wind and being carried higher and higher into the blue.

Cotton, a tea towel dustbunny, thought the down seeds dancing in the sun were just the prettiest things he ever did see. Twirling and tipping, spinning and jostling, the down seeds were nothing like the samey old lumps of tea towel, dishcloth, packaging and paper towels usually seen moping around the kitchen, heavy with airborne fat, decorated with dirt and scrapings. The down seed threads were slender, elegant, straight and true. In the sunshine they shone, in the air they danced and, as they settled, they held out their symmetrical filaments to him and Cotton was helpless.

Bedazzled, he rolled into their midst, but cared not. They gathered closely all around him, mute, gentle and soft and started to sway. Surrounded by beauty, Cotton felt the weight leave his threads and could feel himself being pulled upwards into the blue. It was only after seeing the kitchen door go by that Cotton was shaken from his ecstatic reverie. Suddenly very attentive to his surroundings, Cotton saw the door shrink below and behind him. Fearful and amazed, he realised he was looking down at the windows, roof and chimney of the entire dust bunny domain; the whole house, so big, yet shrinking.

As the down seeds carried him higher, he could see gardens now, lots of them; a blanket of green jungles full of mystery, home to the mindless indifferent insects that occasionally would ravage a dust bunny enclave. Cotton's gaze went beyond the greenery of the retreating gardens and, as he rose higher, was granted a vision stretching far across rooftops and gardens, houses, trees and roads. Above and around him now was the sky.

It was quiet up here. Not a sound from the down seed. Everything below looked so small. The biggest thing Cotton could see was the horizon line, where the land met the sky. No humble tea towel dust bunny had ever conceived of such a thing, let alone seen it for themselves. His world expanding with his altitude, Cotton was spun around in his cage of down seed and he saw there was a horizon everywhere in a vast circle around him. Beyond that, who knew what? Cotton couldn't wait to get back and tell every bunny in the house about this.

RAYON THE DUST BUNNY AND A VACUUM ABHORRED

CHAPTER 12

The arrival of The Vera caused a massive atmospheric commotion. In addition to The Mum sweeping through the kitchen at surprisingly high speed to open the front door, The Mum and The Vera had coalesced into each other laughing and crying, coats and dressing gowns aflap. After much oohing and squeezing at the front door, they moved inside, The Mum's pregnancy bump throwing off great, slowly-spiralling wakes every time she turned. The front door was left open for an age as luggage was ferried from taxi to house in several trips. With some heaving and ho-ing by both The Mum and The Vera, bags and cases were bumped and hauled upstairs into the spare room, where The Vera's encumbrances were dumped without ceremony on the floor.

The outdoor Wind whooshed around with a final flourish as the front door was closed. Instead of rushing straight through the house, purging all dust bunnies in its path, The Wind just buffeted from wall to wall, ceiling to floor, like a cow on a trampoline, then fizzled out.

Having been lofted this way and that by the well-stirred air currents, the lighter dust bunnies in the downstairs rooms were settling slowly, lots of them, sparkling picturesquely as they fell, defining the rays of morning sunshine. A few of the denser clumps had aggregated together in wind-borne collisions into ultra-dust bunnies, almost the size of tennis balls, and had rolled into the low pressure areas and slack air zones and were now immobilised by their own bulk.

As for Rayon, he was swept off his temporary mooring place when The Andrew came downstairs and gallumphed by to say 'hello' to his aunt. Still dizzy from before, Rayon was spun round another few dozen times by the passing Andrew's turbulence and dumped on the floor amongst all the feet. Dangerous place to be for a dust bunny, amongst feet; The Andrew's bare feet could easily snag up quite a sizable clutch of dust bunnies between those porky fat toes. The Mum's furry slippers weren't quite as grabby, but there was still the threat of a major squishing. The Vera's substantial and chunky-soled footwear was an unknown threat, but at least the heavy lugs of the outdoorsy tread gave a dust bunny a fifty/fifty chance in the event of a squishing, better than risking The Mum's slippers by far.

Above, all was small talk. 'Haven't you grown? What was it like in Australia? Have you had the place decorated? Come and have a coffee.'

Back down at floor level amongst the feet and footwear, a familiar voice reached Rayon.

'I thought I told you not to stop there, you dizzy pellet.'

'I haven't really stopped yet,' replied Rayon. 'The walls are still rotating. Wait a minute.' Rayon put out a few threads to steady himself and turned to see Stour peering out at him from in between the chunky sole lugs of The Vera's boots.

'Give a push and get yourself over here,' said Stour. 'You've seen what happens when you linger out in the open.'

Rayon was actually quite pleased to see Stour, even if he had called him a pellet. He was less pleased about traversing the open space between him and Stour with so many feet heaving around him.

'Is it safe?' asked an unconvinced Rayon.

'Safer under here than out there, mate. You can't get squished by yon flipper foot under here,' replied Stour waving a thread towards The Andrew's sprawling bare feet.

Only half convinced, Rayon rolled quickly and warily over to Stour and wriggled his way in between the rubbery bits of The

RAYON THE DUST BUNNY AND A VACUUM ABHORRED

Vera's footwear.

'It's a bit snug.'

'Yeah, the carpet pile does creep up between the gaps and gives you a bit of a squeeze. You're still spherical, aren't you?'

'Mostly, I suppose. What about Knickers and Twill? Where are they?' asked the slightly oblate Rayon.

'I saw them blow by when the front door opened,' replied Stour. 'But they were tumbling rather than flying, so I'm sure they'll have snagged on somewhere.'

On The Vera's arrival, The Wind had forcibly snagged Twill and Knickers onto the industrial-strength nylon straps of The Vera's luggage. Subsequently, both of them were hauled upstairs to the spare room. The bumps of the stairs hadn't dislodged them and, after a partial squishing when the luggage was put down, Twill and Knickers found themselves squeezed a bit tighter than was quite proper, but nevertheless safe, in a nice, dark canyon in between items of The Vera's baggage.

'Well,' said Knickers after it went quiet. 'Blimey.'

'Couldn't agree more,' replied Twill, but obviously thinking about something else. 'You know, it'd be handy to have Stour and that Rayon of yours around to do a recce.'

'He's not my Rayon,' said Knickers a bit too quickly. 'But yes, a wrecky. What's a wrecky?'

'Reconnaisance. Nosey about a bit, look in cupboards, peek round hems. The arrival of this Vera changes everything. We need a sitrep,' said Twill in that firm, decisive way of his that made Knickers' threads tingle a bit, even if she didn't know what he meant.

'We do?' said Knickers.

'Situation report. What tribes are deployed where, strategic analysis of the people's movements, tactical threat assessment, any central vac intel, mop or duster mobilisations, probability of a preemptive tidy-up. That sort of thing,' explained Twill.

I could listen to him talk like that all day, thought Knickers dreamily to herself.

'Oh, of course,' she said, shaking herself to attention. 'Yes. Sitpert. Definitely.'

'So, come on then.'

'What? Who mentioned moving?'

'I did. You, me, recce. There's nobunny else around.'

I *know,* thought Knickers. *Just you, me and this nice, dark secluded canyon...*

'Send us! Send us!' said a keen little voice from above. 'We'll go wrecky. There's lots of us, so we can go wrecky wrecky wrecky wrecky wrecky wrecky... oops.'

A cascade of fluff buried Knickers and Twill under a writhing, giggling mound of fuzzballs, who hadn't yet learnt to keep their threads to themselves.

'Get off, get off!' insisted Knickers as she wriggled her way out from under. 'And you, get your threads out of there,' she added giving a particularly inquisitive fuzzball a hearty snap with a flicked thread.

Twill emerged from under the semi-transparent cloud of fuzzballs, but they didn't seem to stick to Twill the way they did to Knickers. Knickers plucked the last of the fuzzballs from her threads, gave it a push and told it sternly to stay.

'I wondered where this lot had got to,' humphed Knickers. 'I thought we'd seen the last of them when the back door opened.'

'Yes, they do get around a bit,' answered Twill looking around at the fog of fuzzballs surrounding them both. 'They're very mobile, aren't they?'

Knickers caught his train of thought. 'You're not thinking of sending fuzzballs on an intelligence mission, are you?'

'Well, they are mobile and unobtrusive.'

RAYON THE DUST BUNNY AND A VACUUM ABHORRED

'And devoid of all intelligence.'

'We are not devoided,' objected a fuzzball close to Knickers. 'We do so know a thing.'

Knickers rounded on the fuzzball and loomed over it.

'What? What do you know, you pointless particle? You've been blown round the house once by The Wind and you think you know it all already.'

'We know The Mum's going to empty her wardrobe of all her old clothes and give them to The Vera. So there!' retorted the plucky little fuzzball.

'You're just making that up,' said Knickers. 'How could you possibly know that?'

'Because we've been blown round the house once and now we know it all. We know what's going on everywhere because we're everywhere and you're not.'

'Pish and tosh,' exclaimed Knickers. 'Your lot couldn't think your way out of a cardboard tube.'

'Could so, if we all thunked about it the same time.'

'You'd get lost.'

'Wait, wait wait,' interrupted Twill.' What do you mean "*if we all thunked about it at the same time*"?'

'Well,' replied the fuzzball, 'we don't have many thinks, but if we need a Big Think we share it.'

'Share it?'

'Oh yes, we don't have many original thinky thoughts, so we have to share the good ones.'

'How can you share a thought when you're all in different places?' asked a skeptical Twill.

'Oh, we're not really in different places,' said the fuzzball. 'We're just spread out in one big space.'

'You mean you're all joined up?' asked a bewildered Knickers, who'd only ever been in one place at any one time.

'Oh yes. We are all entangled together at the same time, so it doesn't matter how far apart we are. It's all one big think for us.'

'So you lot, you know what's happening everywhere?'

'Of course. Well, anywhere there's a fuzzball.'

'Prove it,' replied Knickers.

'The Mum and The Vera are coming upstairs.'

'Rubbish, I can't hear a thing.'

Just then they felt and heard The Mum and The Vera setting foot on the creaky bottom stair and The Vera laughing out 'All hands to the buttocks and heave'.

'Spooky,' whispered Knickers, slightly in awe.

The Mum and The Vera plodded upstairs in a slow lockstep and went into the main bedroom.

'What are they doing now?' asked Twill.

'Let's see,' replied the fuzzball. 'Looking at doors. Big doors, big doors open. Oooh, pretty colours.'

Twill had it worked out in a jiffy.

'That's the wardrobe. The Mum's instigated a Level 5 archival purge in the main bedroom. For the love of mank, is nowhere safe?'

RAYON THE DUST BUNNY AND A VACUUM ABHORRED

CHAPTER 13

Rayon and Stour's relocation to the main bedroom was a source of great confusion to Rayon. Before being marched upstairs, jammed into the chunky soles of The Vera's rugged footwear, Stour had been making plans for them.

'It's not safe down here,' he said. 'We need to head upstairs. The people always tidy downstairs first to impress the visitors and create a thin veneer of respectability. Then they'll do the stairs and the bathroom. After that, they give up all hope. We'll be safer in one of the bedrooms, the one where The Mum and The Dad roost. That'll be the quietest for a while. Let's go.'

And right then, on cue, The Vera went.

Rayon didn't yet understand dust bunny mobility. He couldn't figure out how dust bunnies got where they wanted to be. Random luck, wasn't it? Go where The Wind blows. Or, did Stour somehow know The Wind would be going that way and made plans to tag along? Or did The Wind sometimes do the dust bunnies' bidding? But dust bunnies couldn't make people do things, could they?

Either way, The Vera's boots transported them upstairs and into the main bedroom. Under The Mum's orders, The Vera undid and removed her boots amidst a flurry of apologies for being a thoughtless oaf. Rayon and Stour wriggled free from the tread of The Vera's boots, just as The Mum started exhuming armfuls of clothes from the wardrobe and piling them high on the bed.

With every piece of clothing pulled from the wardrobe, The Mum and The Vera would go off into rhapsodies of nostalgia about when The Mum wore this or that. With all the flapping and trying on, showers of various designer dust bunnies, released from a long dormancy, fluttered to the floor around Rayon and Stour, anxious to re-acquaint themselves with long lost companions.

'Dahling, I haven't seen you in an eternity,' said one designer dust bunny. 'Where have you been? You absolutely must tell me everything.'

'Well,' said Stour. 'It's been busy.'

'Not you, you button hole. Tuxedo! Tuxedo!'

A perfectly groomed and gorgeous dust bunny was frantically waving a thread over the top of Stour. Her threads were rich, glowing shades of gold, red and lustrous blues, shot through with dashes of verdant green. The effect would have been dazzling but for the bit of sticky barcode label on her right side.

Oh, never been called that before, thought Stour. Discount designer wear; all label and no content.

Rayon was bumped aside by a black ball of a dust bunny, svelte matt black on the inside, polished on the outside. It rolled up to the multi-hued Hermes and they made '*mwah*' noises at each other.

'You are still looking beyond fabulous,' said Tuxedo as they both linked threads and rolled back a bit to admire each other.

'Well, I try,' said Hermes. 'Very dapper yourself. Still not a particle sullying your perfection.'

'Too kind, too kind.'

'Where do you suppose we are all going?' asked Hermes, who had finally redirected some of her attention from herself to her surroundings and started looking around.

'Out, by the look of things,' replied Tuxedo. 'And isn't that all that matters? I haven't had anybunny but business suit and sensible skirt dust bunnies to talk to. Hugo's still banging on.'

A smooth, bottle green dust bunny rolled past Hermes and Tuxedo in conversation with another dust bunny, who looked like it was trying to get away.

RAYON THE DUST BUNNY AND A VACUUM ABHORRED

'So I said, going forward, let's blue sky our media options then focus group the optimised core messaging to each cohort of our stakeholders. Then, if the cat licks it up, we can run up the flag for a regionalised triple tranche rollout in a drip irrigation strategy and see if anybody salutes it.'

'See?' said Tuxedo.

'Poor thing, how dull for you. Never mind, we should have some idea of where we're going when she starts trying on outfits. I do hope it's a party and not a wedding.'

'Too late,' replied Tuxedo. 'Even the wedding dress is getting an outing.'

As The Mum held up the billowing confection of whiteness to herself in front of the mirror, a snowfall of identical wedding dress dust bunnies tumbled to the floor and started wailing.

'Why is she never happy to see us?' they sobbed. 'Why does she always cry?'

'Quick, let's escape before we have to explain,' said Tuxedo. 'Look! There's Dinky. And Burberry, Chanel and... my, my, even refugees from the Eighties. Isn't that Lycra and those annoying little legwarmer pills?'

'Yoo hoo!' hooted Hermes, waving a thread again. 'There's a bit of Izzy, too. Come on, Tuxxy, let's mingle. I wonder what the grand occasion might be?'

Hermes and Tuxedo pushed past Stour and headed for the biggest clumps of newly-arrived designer dust bunnies. Rayon rolled over to join Stour as he watched them roll away.

'Aren't you going to tell them?' asked Rayon.

'I'm sorely tempted not to,' replied Stour.

'Who are those two with the weirdo threads and clashing colours?'

'Oh, that's Westwood and Gaultier. I think they're having an ugly competition.'

'Come on, you two. Join in.'

A lime-green Lycra had bounced over to them and was now bouncing on the spot, waving her threads up and down. 'And one. And two. And step. And reach.'

Orderly rows of day-glo legwarmer pills were bouncing up and down around Rayon and Stour, stretching their threads this way and that in time with Lycra.

'Feel the burn,' insisted Lycra.

'I'm trying to avoid that,' said Stour.

'I'd rather not, thank you,' said Rayon.

'Give it a hundred and ten per cent,' went Lycra.

'Give it up dear, more like,' said Stour dragging Rayon away to somewhere less enthusiastic. 'You're right, we have to tell them.'

Stour looked around at the exquisite diversity of colour and the lofty quality of the threads.

'But they make me feel like pocket lint,' said Stour abstractedly.

'You're not lint, you're a bit of everything,' said Rayon. 'You're very well-rounded.'

'Nice of you to say so,' replied Stour, 'but I still don't think they'll listen to me. I'm too common. At least you're a weird colour. You could almost fit right in with a bit of grooming and a sprig of tinsel.'

'Oh, thank you so much,' replied Rayon. 'Hey, what are you doing?'

'Go on, go on,' said Stour, giving Rayon an encouraging shove over to where Hermes and Tuxedo had joined a large cluster of well-groomed and attractive dust bunnies. The air was filled with excited chatter.

'Excuse me, can I have your attention please?' tried Rayon in his best polite voice.

'Oh, is it time for nibbles?' said an evening wear dust bunny, who was the only one polite enough to respond.

'No. I'm trying to get everybunny's attention.'

RAYON THE DUST BUNNY AND A VACUUM ABHORRED

'Aren't we all, dear thing, aren't we all?' replied the dust bunny.

'Have you tried shouting? I hear that works very well.'

Rayon hadn't tried shouting yet. However, when he did, it didn't work because an outbreak of noisy '*haw haw hawing*' drowned him out completely.

Then, a flimsy creation sashayed over to Rayon. She was entangled from dark, sheer fabrics and Rayon couldn't help but notice he could see through her threads.

'My, aren't you rugged?' she purred. 'Aztec mountainwear? Andy from the Andes. Rough, tough Tommy Tweed, perhaps? But no, the colour gives you away. Santa Fe blanket. Tell me you're a Santa Fe blanket from cowboy country.'

'Errm, Rayon, actually. From a hat.'

'A real alpaca farmer's hat, then? It's the ethnic colours. I'm so into ethnic crafts.'

The way she kept wriggling while she spoke unsettled Rayon in ways he rather liked.

'No, The Josh's hat,' he replied. 'Who are you?'

'Ooh, aren't you bold and forward?' said the dust bunny. 'I'm Silky. I'm woven from naturally produced threads of protein. Isn't that exotic? But enough about me, let's talk about you. What do you think of my lacy bits?'

Rayon sensed the conversation had gone a bit off-topic, but didn't particularly care when Stour tutted and rolled over to interrupt and also have a secret, closer look at Silky.

'All right, all right, I'll do it.' Stour puffed himself up. 'OI, YOU LOT. QUIET!'

Rayon was quite impressed when it did go quiet.

'This isn't a social!' yelled Stour to a rippling '*aww*' of disappointment. 'It's a tidy up. The central vac gets fixed tomorrow! And some of you are heading for the consignment store!'

It took Stour and Rayon about half an hour to reconstitute their proper shape after the stampede of designer dust bunnies, all heading for the dark under the bed, crushed them underthread.

As The Mum and The Vera fussed over the few remaining fashion relics, Rayon and Stour watched desperate designer dust bunnies being carried along, stricken with indecision: stay and face the tidy up, or leave and face the cruel ignominy of being deeply, deeply discounted?

Hardly a dust bunny fell to the floor now. The last few designer dust bunnies ousted from the safe, dark obscurity of the back of the wardrobe were clinging on to clothes destined for the consignment store, while others were caught up in the folding of the clothes taken through to The Vera's room to be packed into a spare suitcase. Either way, their time in this house was over and their future was fraught with social and existential uncertainty.

With the The Mum's bedroom so seriously inundated with dust bunnies – the bright, colourful, obvious kind, Stour added pointedly – they should try and find somewhere safer. So, when The Vera took another armful of The Mum's abandoned fashions to pack into her suitcase, Rayon and Stour hitched onto The Vera's stout woolly socks and were whisked to the spare room in a few paces. They then unhitched from The Vera's socks and rolled into the relative safety of the darkness under the bed.

After adding her armful of clothes to the pile already on the bed, The Vera took up her spare suitcase, opened it, peered in the corners, sniffed inside, then flipped the case over to give it a shake to get the loose bits out.

The bits were dust bunnies The Vera had taken on holiday. They'd been to places, seen things. And now, newly released into the wild, they glided down over and around Rayon and Stour, clapping when they landed as if this had never happened before. In the tussle on the floor there was an outbreak of apologising, re-arranging of threads and the establishing of whereabouts.

RAYON THE DUST BUNNY AND A VACUUM ABHORRED

'Oh dear, I think she's gone two-star.'
'It's chilly, too.'
'Listen; no music.'
'A bit light on carefree chatter, too.'
'What's the nightlife like I wonder?'
'Look,' said a lurid fluorescent green beach towel dust bunny pointing a thread at Rayon. 'There's a native in costume. Let's ask him.'

A. MICHAEL COLLINS

CHAPTER 14

When The Vera hoisted her suitcase for inspection and a shake, Knickers, Twill and sundry drifts of tenuous fuzzballs were suddenly left horribly exposed on the open floor. Then, The Wind rushed in to where the case used to be and tumbled them over the carpet until they ran into a bed leg, coming to a halt all in a knot. Reluctantly pulling herself away from a delicious 'accidental' tangle with Twill, Knickers looked around to get her bearings. It was curiously quiet. The fuzzballs were strangely un-annoying, staying close, being quiet, bunching up closer still when a clutch of tourist dust bunnies tumbled by, staring, yoo-hooing and waving.

Not only were the drifts of fuzzballs clustering close around her and Twill, but Knickers could see scores of designer dust bunnies rolling around aimlessly on the floor, entirely disorientated by being in a non-retail or social environment. There were dozens of creamy, freshly-entangled, high-threadcount bedsheet dust bunnies, plainly visible all around the bed, the aroma of sea-fresh fabric softener now on the air. Around the walls, the regular spare room dust bunnies, that had so easily escaped the Dad's perfunctory cleaning efforts, were bunched up higher than ever before. Now, to make things even worse, there were a suitcaseful of tourists.

'Twill,' said Knickers, 'that sitrep thing. This isn't a good one, is it? Target-rich and threat imminent, and all that stuff?'

'No, not good. Not good at all,' agreed Twill. 'Fuzzballs, is it like this all over the house?'

'Is this a quiz?' replied one fuzzball. 'We're not very good at quizzes.'

RAYON THE DUST BUNNY AND A VACUUM ABHORRED

'No, it's just a question – is it like this all over the house?'

'Oh no, the walls are different colours. Is there a prize now?'

Twill had to put out a thread to keep a growling Knickers away from the fuzzball.

'No, no prizes.'

'Points. We like points. Can we have points?'

'I'll point you on a nice, sharp spindle...' said Knickers.

'Yes, there are points,' said Twill patiently. 'But only if you answer the questions. Are there lots of dust bunnies? Everywhere? All over?'

The nearest fuzzball stopped bobbing for moment and looked like it was listening.

'Yes.'

'Yes what?'

'Yes, dust bunnies all over, silly. How many points? How many points do we get?'

'Eleventy three.'

'Woo hoo.'

'Bonus points if you can tell me where the most dust bunnies are,' continued Twill. 'Which room?'

'That's easy. The Andrew's bedroom, the big one's bedroom, the spare room, the stairs, the living room, behind all the screens, where the coats are, in the kitchen and the laundry room.'

'But that's everywhere,' objected Knickers. 'You can't have the most ever dust bunnies everywhere.'

'Tis so, too.'

'Are you saying that every room is filled with the most bunnies ever?' echoed Twill, trying to tease out some meaning from the fuzzballs' answers.

'Maximum capacity. Eighty-three thousand, five hundred and forty-seven points, please.'

'What?'

'One for every dust bunny in the house, of course,' said the fuzzball. 'Look, there's your blue friend.'

Further along under the bed, Rayon and Stour were being harangued by the tourist dust bunnies. They were bickering about the level of service in this establishment and wanting to know where they were expected to spend the night, when it was obvious these posh and brassy designer dust bunnies had nabbed all the good spots. Not that the good spots were all that good in the first place, they added sniffily. Rayon and Stour were trapped by whining tourists and were coiling up tightly under the onslaught.

Twill quickly rolled over and put on his best announcement voice.

'Visitors, recent arrivals, welcome, welcome. If you've just arrived with The Vera's luggage, can you make your way round the back of that suitcase over there, where someone will make sure your every need is taken care of. Thank you.'

Twill waved a thread to show them the way. The tourist dust bunnies responded with unthinking compliance and dutifully formed a neat queue, then led themselves away to temporary security behind a suitcase under the bed.

'Yes, that suitcase, over there,' directed Twill. 'Moving right along. Thank you. Thank you.'

'Come on, you two, this way,' and he began hustling Rayon and Stour in exactly the opposite direction.

'Thank you for rescuing us, but who's meeting them behind the suitcase?' asked a puzzled Rayon as they all bobbed back to join Knickers and the fuzzballs by the bed leg.

'No-one,' answered Twill.

'Then, what you said was...' went on Rayon, slowly joining the dots because he'd never heard a fib before.

'A dirty filthy lie, that's what,' replied Twill. 'And aren't you glad I told it? It was them or you.'

RAYON THE DUST BUNNY AND A VACUUM ABHORRED

Reunited under the bed, Twill insisted everybunny, fuzzballs too, should hunker down as close as they could to the carpet and find a loop to hang on to.

When they were all anchored in the relative security of an old carpet crater, Rayon waved a thread at the dust bunny-laden landscape.

'Look at this,' he said. 'All our talk of central vac has done nothing but stir things up. We've just made things worse by warning everybunny. Yarn said we should do nothing and he was right.'

'Yarn was right in another way,' pointed out Knickers. 'Dust is prevailing.'

'He's good at being right in a useless way, that Yarn,' added a disgruntled Stour. 'Maybe it would be better if he was wrong more often.'

'I suppose we will find out tomorrow,' answered Rayon.

Household atmospheric conditions remained lively throughout the day. The Mum and The Dad and The Vera swished up, down and around the house, but turbulence was manageable – even when The Andrew blundered through every room downstairs to meet and greet parents and aunt before stomping back upstairs and falling onto his bed like felled lumber ready to conquer Level 4. The effect on the resident bed dust bunnies of The Andrew's backside-to-mattress impact was more mechanical than meteorological. Instead of being scooped up by The Wind and tossed about, the bed dust bunnies were catapulted through high, arcing parabolas, landing close to where they were launched from, unharmed but a bit fuzzier and windswept around the edges after their high acceleration launch.

Dinnertime saw another front of domestic weather move through when the cooking started. Localised domestic turbulence was at a slighty higher level than usual due to the unexpected emergence of a tablecloth and napkins ('Let's go posh,' The Mum had said). The flapping of the tablecloth stirred up sudden, short-lived gusts and darting eddies in the dining room. Then there were the usual draughts, vortices, gusts and flaps from the people swanning about, as well as the potent but short-lived gales from various cupboard, microwave, fridge and oven doors being hastily yanked open, then slammed shut.

After dinner and a flurry of cleaning up, dust bunny displacement and disruption levels declined to a low for the day. The last event was the eruption of several geysers of intra-cushion sofa dust bunnies when The Mum, The Dad, The Andrew and The Vera fell back into the embrace of the sofa and comfy chairs for an evening's televisioning.

At yawning o'clock, there was a collective heaving and groaning as everyone hoisted themselves vertical for the final assault on the stairs to bed. The Mum was assisted upwards by a laughing Dad and The Vera and The Andrew singing 'Yo-o heave ho, yo-o heave ho' at every slow, ponderous step. After swapping good nights, hugs and mwahs at the top of the stairs, The Mum and The Dad, The Vera and The Andrew went their separate ways.

Eventually, the sloshing, clatter and banging of people abluting, finding pyjamas, getting the next day's clothes out and general pre-bed faffing about slowly settled. Doors latched snugly shut, bedside lamps clicked on, overhead lights clicked off, blankets and sheets adjusted to taste, pillows fluffed, books taken up, pages found and silence descended.

In the spare room, Rayon, Knickers, Twill and Stour huddled in a solemn half-shadowed group by the bedside table leg, lit from above by the bedside light. The locals and the tourists had come to an uneasy truce and space had been found for them somewhere.

It was Knickers who startled them out of their silent ruminations about the day's events and the events to come.

'We forgot about the bathroom dust bunnies.'

RAYON THE DUST BUNNY AND A VACUUM ABHORRED

'Oh,' said Twill.

'Ah,' said Stour.

'What?' said Rayon.

'The bathroom dust bunnies,' replied Knickers. 'Nobody told them about the central vac.' Was that a hint of annoyance or guilt in her tone?

'Bathroom dust bunnies?' said Rayon. 'Isn't it too wet? For dust bunnies?'

'Only in parts. There are dry patches on the higher grounds, a safe distance from the swampy mires,' explained Twill.

'But where do they come from?' asked Rayon.

'Towels, facecloths, bathmats, laundry, undergarments...' replied Stour.

'Not that there's anything wrong with that,' interrupted Knickers. 'Bathroom dust bunnies. They're cotton. Mostly.'

'Mostly, but not all,' said Stour pointedly. 'Tell Rayon about the rest of it. Go on.'

'Well, there's the toilet paper fibres.'

'And...?' prompted Stour again.

'Well, they're sort of more organic.'

'Like a hundred per cent organic cotton?' offered Rayon helpfully.

'More like organism.'

'Like alive?'

'Oh, for muck's sake,' said Knickers giving up the fight. 'No, they're not like us. They have, you know, bits. People bits stuck to them. Skin cell bits. Like desiccated coconut on a white chocolate truffle sort of bitty. Scabs sometimes. Toenail clippings. Earwax. And then there are the hairs. Oh, untangle me now, so many different kinds of hairs. Long ones, short ones, even some stout, curly ones. And airborne particulates.' Knickers stressed the way she said airborne particulates to let Rayon know that a fuller description might not be welcome.

'Yuck, stop. I get it,' said Rayon. 'But shouldn't we tell them anyway?'

'You go, then.'

'Mmm, well, I'd like to,' replied Rayon quickly, 'but, em, I'm new here…Perhaps somebunny more experienced?'

'Nope,' said Kickers.

'Nope,' said Twill.

'Nope,' said Stour.

'They're on their own, then? You're abandoning them?'

'You didn't volunteer to go, either,' Stour reminded Rayon. 'You're abandoning the bathroom dust bunnies just as much as we are.'

'It's the bits, isn't it?' asked Twill gently. 'The scabs, toenail clippings, skin debris and those airborne particulates.'

'The minging clart,' added Stour for clarity.

'Yes,' came Rayon's small, shameful answer.

'Me too,' agreed Stour. 'Just the notion gives me the dry boak.'

'We all feel the same way about the bathroom dust bunnies, Rayon,' Twill explained. 'Conflicted. We feel an obligation to help, but ashamed at having absolutely no sincere desire to help. Is it something like that?'

'Yes, exactly,' exclaimed a much-relieved Rayon.

'Well, don't waste your time arguing with yourself,' replied Twill. 'Tomorrow we might all be in the same garbage bag, forewarned or not.'

Meanwhile, four feet seven inches, or one hundred and thirty nine centimeters above Rayon's ethical dilemma, the fuzzballs perching around the upper rim of the reading light lampshade were watching The Vera intently, for they'd never seen one before. Awake, she was very boring; sleeping, she was much more fun. The Vera was a snorer.

RAYON THE DUST BUNNY AND A VACUUM ABHORRED

In with the fresh air, out with old. The prodigious vibrations of The Vera's respiratory structures shook a gawking, too-curious fuzzball from the lampshade. It fell towards The Vera's open mouth until, to its immense relief and ensuing delight, another rattling exhalation launched the fortunate fuzzball upwards again and kept it momentarily suspended in mid-air. Another downward rush on the inhalation, almost to the point of no return from a soggy, salivary ending, only to be re-launched again upwards; this time, however, it would go toppling off the topmost reaches of the snore, almost delirious with glee, landing back on the top of the lampshade.

'Again. Again.'

Another emboldened fuzzball leapt from the lampshade. It floated into the main current of the snore, then it too was lofted upwards. Down, then up; down, then up. Another joined in, and another until there was a small flock of fuzzballs snore-riding in the moonlight.

The fun stopped when the boundless and thoughtless enthusiasm of one particularly translucent and lightweight fuzzball caused it to badly mis-time its launch. It fell straight into The Vera's mouth, making her ack and gag as she tried, half asleep, to dislodge the sodden fuzzball from the back of her throat. Finally, to the horror of the watching fuzzballs, she swallowed hard, rolled on to her side and went back to sleep.

A. MICHAEL COLLINS

CHAPTER 15

Mr X (name redacted to protect the partially innocent from the wrath of the justifiably outraged) was not a bad man. Many knew him as a kind, honest man, fun with the kids, good with animals, polite and punctual. A gentleman indeed. He himself would be the first to admit he was not a genius, but he was good with his hands. He took care to load up his van with all the supplies and tools he might need for that morning's central vac job – screwdrivers, wrenches, saws, needle-nose pliers for pulling out bits and pieces from those hard-to-reach places, and keen blades to cut away the accumulated hair that always, always found a way to wrap itself around the bit that spins.

He'd also be bringing tools to assess the health of its electro-mechanical heart; a meter for ohms, volts and amps, wires, plugs and crocodile clips with their savage little teeth. He'd pack tubing, patches and adhesives to repair tears, splits or cracks in its tubular innards and writhing metal snakes, tightly coiled, to force down the gullet of the central vac to dislodge any stubborn obstructions in its tracts. From the Department of Redundancy Department, he would bring a small portable vacuum cleaner to vacuum clean the vacuum cleaner. A handy man indeed, was Mr X. Every eventuality considered.

To a dust bunny, though, Mr X was the devil's opposable thumb.

On the morning of the central vac repair, nothing yet stirred in the house. In The Andrew's bedroom, a nosey, early morning sun edged through the gap between the curtains to illuminate an unusual lack of debris on the floor; no laundry, no dust bunnies.

RAYON THE DUST BUNNY AND A VACUUM ABHORRED

The creeping light of dawn spread a bit further over the floor, almost to The Andrew's bed. Still nothing. With the sun rising just a few degrees higher, bold beams of sunlight flashed into being, suddenly dispelling the gloom under the bed.

The unwelcome light of day suddenly illuminated the great assembly of dust bunnies of all tribes and fibres crowding close together on the floor and banked high up around the walls, all seeking sanctuary under the bed. All winced and cursed silently at the sudden brightness, condemned now to do nothing but wait with great trepidation to see what transpired.

In every room, the massed ranks of dust bunnies all cowered and listened fretfully for clues and portents. The doorbell rang.

The Dad was an early riser so he opened the door. Mr X introduced himself as the central vac repair man and The Dad invited him in. Coming in with Mr X, a parcel of Wind weaseled its way into the house. However, it was too early in the morning for high jinks, so The Wind simply ruffled the accumulated dust bunnies, making thousands of them shimmy and wobble as one. But the movement, the nervous agitation, rippled through the tribes in all their hiding places. Is this it? Is this it?

The Dad helped Mr X with his tools and instruments and closed the door. At floor level by the front door, grey clouds of mottled clumps and dense mats of dust bunnies watched in solemn silence as The Dad led Mr X past them and down into the dark, cluttered lair of the central vac in the basement.

Downstairs, the basement dust bunnies watched as The Dad and Mr X passed their recesses and cubbyholes. Mostly entangled from rough and ready work clothes and industrial-strength fibres, threads and filaments, these were ill-groomed dust bunnies of few words and fewer thoughts. But the mood of the house had reached them, even down here.

'Don't like the look of that.'

'Nope.'

'Arr.'

'Aye.'

'Don't look good at all.'

'Arr.'

'Nope.'

'Aye.'

The Dad guided Mr X to the central vac and left Mr X to his work. Mr X placed his tools and equipment tidily around the body of the central vac; the smaller portable vacuum cleaner to his right, his box of diabolical instruments to his left. It was shadowy and dark in the basement, so he hung a work lamp above him for better illumination.

Mr X knelt in front of the central vac unit, peering to see what the model number and year was. He gave the central vac a quick start up, just to hear how it whined, but his innocent curiosity ignited a quake of shivering fear in the dust bunnies around the house. The return of the central vac! So quickly? The sound of the central vac shutting down abated their fear only slightly – it was now a matter of when, not if.

Even without any great particular heft or density, the dust bunnies Rag, Dungaree and Sockjam were smart enough to know they were watching something extraordinary when Mr X stood up, did something with his hands at the throat of the central vac, then pulled its head off. Mr X had extracted the heart of the central vac – its inner windings and coils, the very lungs and lights of the thing.

Mr X inspected the motor unit for only a moment before nodding to himself and reaching for his faithful portable vacuum cleaner.

Screaming enthusiastically into action, Mr X thrust its screeching nozzle deep into the central vac's motor unit to remove the years of accumulated oily mung clogging the windings. Mr X's fastidious nature was only satisfied when he finally saw the gleaming copper wires of the central vac's heart and the strong, grey steel of its ribs.

He checked the bearings for wear – no wiggle or stiffness there. His seasoned eye inspected the coils and windings and he shone a bright light on the rotors and points of electrical contact.

Turning his attention to the circulatory systems of the central vac, Mr X placed the motor unit to one side before re-installing it. That proved catastrophic for Rusty, a dust bunny made of unravelled overall and, tragically, a sliver of wire wool. The mighty magnets of the central vac's motor plucked up Rusty by the wires and clasped him close to their rotors, condemning him to be interred into the carcass of the central vac. Rusty's predicament did not go unnoticed, however.

'See that?'

'Arr!'

'Yup!'

'Aye!'

'Don't look good at all.'

'Nope.'

'Yup.'

'Arr.'

Mr X replaced tired gaskets and blown seals, making sure the new parts were bedded down properly to contain The Wind that blows backwards. With gauged instruments and insulated probes, Mr X checked the amount and pressure of electrons running along the nerves of the central vac to every room in the house. No damage there. To the tubes themselves next; almost certainly a blockage somewhere, but where?

Mr X set about finding the problem. He re-inserted the motor of the unit, clamped it firmly in place and flipped the switch to power it up. Power on, the massive screech of the newly fettled unit shattered the silence all the way to the top of the house, freezing the dust bunnies in stark terror and stirring even the inert Andrew from his slumbers.

Wincing at the noise himself, Mr X tried a test run. He attached the working end of the central vac directly into the body of the central unit. Suddenly, the central vac breathed again, full strength; no feeble, wheezing central vac here. Mr X quickly ran the muzzle of the central vac around the basement floor for a suction test, snatching up clumps of drab cardboard fibre dust bunnies in the blink of an eye. Instantly, he whipped away cascades of colourful and sparkly fancy dress dust bunnies who had just popped out to take a look, curious to know what the screaming was all about.

With no obvious problem between motor and muzzle, Mr X surmised any blockage would be in the hidden bowels of the machine, the maze of tubing running between the walls. Mr X switched the central unit off and a sudden silence filled the basement. *That's a shocking noise, though*, thought Mr X. *I shall have to have a word with the owner about that.*

Mr X then had to go upstairs and find the source of the blockage, carefully checking every outlet in the house to find the obstruction; probe, test and poke, probe, test and poke. After declaring the lounge and hallway clear, Mr X found the obstruction in the kitchen.

The great clot of dishcloth dust bunnies had done a very good job of choking the central vac to death, so it wasn't until Mr X's slender, coiled metal snake was forcibly rammed down the gullet of the central vac outlet that the dishcloth dust bunnies were finally mechanically dislodged from the internal tubing of the central vac, all resistance crushed.

The obstruction cleared, Mr X powered up the central vac and it effortlessly inhaled, in one gulp, the entire bolus of dishcloth dust bunnies, toothpick and all.

The central vac was declared functional and clear.

'Clear, but not healthy,' explained Mr X to The Mum and The Dad. 'That's an old unit, lots of wear and tear. It'll work, but I can't say for how much longer.'

A discussion about replacement costs and installation dates followed. Details of the conversation rippled through the dust bunny communities, sparking off ill-informed conjecture and horror at the thought of a new, improved, nastier central vac, coming soon, no need to pay now.

'Well, we've other things to think about right now,' said The Dad, gently patting The Mum's bump.

'Of course, of course,' agreed Mr X. 'When things get quiet again – maybe in twenty years' time. Ha, ha, ha.'

After a deal of clattering and banging, Mr X returned his tools and equipment to the van, wrote up the bill and left. As the front door closed, The Wind sneaked in one more time to give every-bunny another nasty shake, adding to their already highly increased nervous agitation. The Wind could be surprisingly evil at times.

'Right,' said The Dad, 'let's take this thing for a test drive.'

CHAPTER 16

The Dad hauled the coils of the central vac into the television room and plugged the tail in to the wall socket. The central vac roared back to life, swallowing hundreds of cubic feet, tens of cubic meters of empty air every second. The Dad fitted the dangerous end with a tapering snout and set it loose on the floor. Snatched up first were the plainly visible clumps of dust bunnies sticking out from under the chair legs and around the edges of the couch. Then, the central vac closed in on the thick seam of dust bunnies around the base of the television unit. As The Dad steered the muzzle of the central vac around the perimeter of the television unit, The Wind that blows backwards inhaled the misty grey dust bunnies in a thick, fast-flowing current of fluff, fibre and thread, leaving a broad swathe of barren carpet-scape in its wake.

The Dad set about the couch next, fitting some other form of narrow nozzle to the central vac, then hauling cushions and pillows aside to let the stabbing beak snort up the massed ranks of couch, curtain and carpet dust bunnies – especially those richly-endowed with nutritious particles of toast crumbs, cornflakes, popcorn and other friable and brittle foodstuffs. Not a crumb remained when The Dad finally replaced the cushions and pillows.

Despite hanging on grimly behind heating grilles and vents, the screen and monitor dust bunnies in the television and computer screens were the next to be gobbled up by the beak of the insatiable central vac. The Dad steered the slender, ever-inhaling beak of the central vac around the back of the computer and television, searching out the places where the screen and monitor dust bunnies cowered. As the dust bunnies were caught in the sway of that monstrous Wind, their tenacious anchor threads were quickly strained, then pulled taut before finally being stretched to dislocation. Having lost their grip, the screen and monitor dust bunnies were gobbled up whole and by the hundreds.

Escalating the carnage, The Mum entered, waving a fluffy duster on a stick – a proper duster – at lampshades, ledges, the high tops of curtains, frames and light fittings, launching thin fogs of dust bunnies into the air. The Dad pulled the beak off the central vac and waved the central vac's unfettered nozzle into the clouds of dislodged dust bunnies as swirling, all-consuming, ocean-sized currents of air slurped them all up before they could hit the ground.

The Dad then fitted another head onto the central vac, this time giving it the profile of a hammerhead shark. With this, The Dad assaulted the carpet directly, even the corners. No quarter was given. All the carpet, couch and curtain dust bunnies that survived the first wave were snatched up on this pass. Even the sanctuary of the space beneath the chairs was violated. Seating was either tipped back or shunted aside to serve the central vac's relentless pursuit of its prey. Rugs were lifted and the central vac lay waste to yet another tribe of dust bunnies. Dust bunnies behind the curtains? Snuffed out. Dust Bunnies behind the door? Snuffed out. The Dad backed out of the room, vacuuming as he went and set off for his next destination.

The kitchen dust bunnies, high and low, as a result of The Mum with her duster and The Dad with the central vac, vanished with as little resistance. In an astonishing display of domestic diligence, the fridge was pulled out like an old tooth from between the cupboards and Serviette and his clan were greedily snatched up, parmesan and parsley bits and all. Even the densely-packed cooling coils were sucked clear of any vestige of dust bunny.

After being professionally serviced, the central vac's appetite and capacity was insatiable. Deep-dwelling, cupboard-under-the-stairs dust bunnies didn't even have time to get used to the brightness as the door was thrown open and the central vac snatched them up, plunging them down into a darker kind of darkness.

The usually safe low-pressure and low-traffic areas behind doors and around furniture received unusual amounts of attention because of the sudden over-crowding of refugee dust bunnies trying to find somewhere safe to hide. A sterile, featureless swathe of bleak, empty tidiness was visited upon hallways, doorways, shelving, cupboards, around all the edges and halfway up the stairs before The Mum and The Dad ran out of enthusiasm and energy.

Calling in reinforcements, The Mum dispatched The Andrew upstairs with the coils of the central vac to continue the tidy up and 'to start at the tops and work down, under the beds and things, cupboards and do every room.'

The cacophonous gorging of the central vac had awoken The Vera and she gingerly squeezed past the coils of the central vac to make her way downstairs and to the kitchen. Apologies were made for the noise, but coffee was produced as consolation and The Vera and The Mum removed themselves to talk in the now pristine television room.

Upstairs in The Vera's room, Rayon, Knickers, Twill and Stour, motionless and silent, listened as The Andrew wrestled his way up the stairs, with the body of the central vac coiled in a loving embrace around him.

Rayon, Knickers, Twill and Stour watched from behind a bedside table leg as the door swung open and The Andrew barged in, wielding the head of the central vac. The tail he plugged into the wall socket. Powered up, the black maw of the central vac gobbled up an easy target just for sport – an amorphous clump of variegated dust bunnies, recently displaced from the wardrobe and marooned near the door. Whoomp, gone. Then, remembering his instructions about dutifully starting at the top, The Andrew wrenched the nose off the central vac and, in its place, fitted a bristled attachment. Now it hissed.

With this deadly whiskered head, The Andrew systematically laid waste to the lighter dust bunnies and fuzzballs on lampshades, picture frames and all their lofty perches.

The wardrobe had been cleared of obstructions and the doors thrown open to let the central vac reach right back in to long-unvisited corners, nooks and clefts, where dust bunnies had lain undisturbed for many years. The Andrew turned to them next.

After their long years of patient and slow accumulation at the back of the wardrobe and in innumerable corners and havens, these dense, well-established colonies of dust bunnies, for all their desperately clutching and grasping threads, gained no purchase on the indifferent smoothness of the wardrobe shelves. Instead, they were drawn inexorably towards the central vac as it passed over them, slurping them up on a conveyor belt of air into its ever-open gullet.

After a minute or so, the wardrobe, depending on which end of the central vac you were on, was left either neatly pristine or cruelly devoid of dust bunny.

Directing his attention to the floor, The Andrew capped the central vac with another accessory designed for high volume inhalation. He steered the vacuum head over the carpet, the central vac snatching up rootless dust bunnies mercilessly – and now, very much more effectively. Each sweep of the head cleared a well-defined swathe of extinction through the tribes of dust bunnies scattered across the floor. The Andrew next rammed the central vac's head deep into the carpet trenches of the perimeter, dragging out even the most tenaciously anchored dust bunnies.

Finally, as if sniffing out the trail of a prey animal, the central vac homed in on the dust bunnies under the bed. Kneeling down for extra reach, The Andrew waved the central vac under the bed in sweeping arcs of increasing length and devastation. The closest dust bunnies vanished the fastest, gone in the blink of an eye.

Just beyond the immediate reach of the central vac's relentless intake, dense clumps of dust bunnies began to roll like tumbleweed towards the central vac, borne mercilessly by the perpetual inhalation. They rolled faster and faster, then vanished with a whop, whop sound up the snout of the vacuum. Then, The Dad came in to help and lifted each end of the bed in turn, clear off the floor, giving the central vac unfettered access to the last bastion and sanctuary of the bedroom dust bunnies. In less than a minute, they were gone. Not a dust bunny remained.

Crowded round the base of The Vera's luggage, the long-distance, high-mileage vacation-wear dust bunnies were utterly oblivious. They were having a wonderful time, exaggerating about their travels and travails or boasting about their constituent threads to seem more sophisticated and cosmopolitan.

'I picked up this thread here from the robes of an Egyptian oarsman on a night boat to Cairo,' said one.

'Well, this white thread is from the apron of the patisserie chef of the best hotel in Beijing,' said another. 'Here, smell – that's real vanilla pod, not your artificial synthetic stuff.'

'Oh, is there real synthetic stuff then, too?'

'Pah, locals. You want exotic, I'll give you exotic.' A dust bunny, entangled from outdoorsy clothing, lifted a thread to show them his threadpit. 'Get close, get close, you won't get another chance to see this.'

'I can't see anything.'

'Me neither.'

'Those three smooth brown hairs, all lined up, black on the end?'

'Oh, there. Yes.'

'Duck-billed platypus fur.'

'No.'

'Well, ah've been rinsed in a sheep piss, ye know,' chipped in a rough, tweedy-looking item.

'What's that loud, whooshing noise? Is the house taking off for a flight somewhere?' said another dust bunny.

Then they heard The Dad's voice very close by. 'Let me shift Veras' bags.'

Witnessing the black mouth of the central vac inhaling the tourists, Rayon, Knickers Twill and Stour wondered how much time they had left.

'He's going slower than I expected,' said Twill, shouting over the wind noise. 'But I think he's just being thorough. Won't be long now.'

'So what's our Plan C?' asked Rayon.

'Plan C? We don't have a Plan C. Or D before you ask,' answered Knickers.

'Never mind a paddle, we don't even have a canoe,' said Stour.

'So what do we do now?' asked Rayon, watching the approaching central vac.

'Nothing,' answered Knickers. 'That's all we can do now. Like Yarn told us to.'

CHAPTER 17

A world-filling wind, sudden darkness then the rush upwards, bumping from side to side around the coils of the central vac. But then Rayon's threads caught up with the rest of him as he reached the same speed as the air in the tubes. It was quieter here in the pitch-black entrails of the central vac. The howling shriek of the central vac was more distant, as if buried in tunnels far away. Rayon couldn't judge his speed in the dark, or even if he was moving at all. Then there was a bump and he could feel himself skidding against the sides of the tube, going fast. He clung on hard with all his threads, slowing his descent into the gullet of the central vac by a precious second or two. A pale blue light shone all around him now, getting brighter.

Where's that light coming from? he wondered.

'So, looks like the Biddies were right about you.' That was Knickers' voice yelling at him. Rayon could see Knickers, like him, scrabbling to get some traction on the other side of the tube, and lit up with the same bluish tinge.

'What?'

'You do glow in the dark,' yelled Knickers.

Rayon's desperate friction braking was generating static electricity, making Rayon glow bright blue, his light illuminating their descent through the twists and turns of the central vac's innards. By his own light, Rayon could see Twill and Stour quite clearly now, too.

Suddenly, their rapid passage faltered, the air around them stuttering, slowing down, speeding up, slowing down. The central vac was coughing and spluttering. Far below, the central vac began to whine, as if in agony, choking on something. From far above came The Andrew's voice, floating down the tubes.

'Stupid sock!'

Upstairs, The Andrew wrenched the tail of the central vac from the wall and the tortured cries of the central vac stopped. In the guts of the machine, The Wind that blows backwards stopped. Along the horizontal length of tubes, dust bunnies in airborne transit came to a crumpled, skidding halt. Those dust bunnies in the downward tubes piled up in rapidly growing mounds at the first right-angled bend they encountered. The Dad shouted 'not to plug in the central vac until I say so' and he went down into the basement to see what the problem was.

Even though The Wind that blows backwards had stopped, there was one bundle of dust bunnies that couldn't stop, however hard their threads scrabbled. They tumbled, ever so slowly, over the lip of a bend and started a slow flutter down the last, long section of tube that led into the abyssal, capacious belly of the central vac itself.

In the basement, The Dad lifted the central vac motor from its housing to see whether or not it was full. He peered into the collection bin of the central vac, the final pit from which there was no escape. Thick deposits of dust bunnies stared back.

In the tubes above The Dad, Rayon was still scrabbling hard for traction as he fell down that final shaft. He wasn't slowing down, but was glowing brighter.

Upstairs, The Andrew pulled the guilty sock out of the central vac wall receptacle with a bent coat hanger. Triumphant, he held the sock aloft and shouted down to The Dad.

'I got it! I fixed the central vac, Dad.'

The Andrew then plugged the central vac's tail back into the wall and the motor sprung back to life.

'No, not now!' yelled The Dad as he lunged to replace the motor in the housing, slamming it down hard to make it airtight.

As the lid went down, Twill, Stour, Rayon and Knickers tumbled out of the last length of tubing and into the belly of the central vac.

For a brief instant, Rayon's blue light illuminated his comrades in the bin far below. They were crowded down below, thick as velvet, deep, silent, all looking up at him far too fervently for his liking.

As the highly-charged Rayon fell past the motor assembly, one of his threads brushed against Rusty's outstretched threads. Rusty, the magnetically enslaved dust bunny with a bit of steel in him. The two connected.

Before he was singed to fine ash and an almost imperceptible puff of smoke, there was just enough conductive metal in Rusty to guide Rayon's accumulated charge to where it was needed. A nice big, fat, bright, static electric spark short-circuited the electro-mechanical heart of the central vac motor. The electrical jolt confused the decrepit pitted coils and rotors of the central vac motor sufficiently to convince it that negative was positive and positive was negative. It started going backwards and suck turned to blow.

Last in, first out, Rayon, Twill, Stour and Knickers were amongst the first ejected out of the central vac, so they had a wonderful view of cataracts of dust bunnies streaming out of the central vac receptacles in the walls. In every room of the house, dust bunnies erupted in torrents out of the walls. For a precious few seconds before The Dad recovered his wits, the central vac hosed out dust bunnies to splash and spill against walls, floors and doors, flooding the air with specks, motes, bundles, lumps, clumps and knots; every collective noun of dust bunny inundated the rooms, all the way up to the lampshades.

After their explosive expulsion from the belly of the central vac back into their rightful domain, the tribes of dust bunnies in every room joyously tumbled and whirled through the bright spring

RAYON THE DUST BUNNY AND A VACUUM ABHORRED

sunlight, illuminated and luminous, like glowing, dancing snow.

The panic-stricken Dad switched the electricity off and, with the one and only exhalation the central vac would ever make, the machine sputtered to a halt.

Having just borne witness to the return of the dust bunnies, The Mum stood immobile and silent as dust bunnies settled back gently to the ground around her and on her. She blew an errant dust bunny from the tip of her nose and, with the back of her hand, brushed some more from the top of her bump.

'Oh,' she said. 'Oh!' she said again, this time holding a hand to her belly. 'Oh, oh, oh!' she added but louder this time.

The eruption of dust bunnies was forgotten in the rush to get The Mum to wherever the human equivalent of fuzzballs were hatched. Still swirling up near the kitchen ceiling, Rayon thought he heard *'hops it all'*, but he didn't have time to work out what *'hops it all'* meant before the front door opened and the people rushed out and The Wind swept in.

Sneakily, The Wind also blew the back door open as the front door closed. Boldly now, The Wind in all its forms invited itself in from the garden and danced an entropic tango around the house. Boisterous turbulence, squalls, flurries, gusts and buffeting, whirls, vortices, tourbillions and draughts; eddies (fast and slow), currents, zephyrs and puffs all swept around the house, shepherding the tribes, colonies and communities of displaced dust bunnies back, more or less, to their naturally appointed places.

By the time a helpful neighbour had come by to close the back door, thus excommunicating The Wind, it was as if all the tidying had never happened.

'Again! Again!' cried the fuzzballs, dizzy with turbulence and excitement.

'Isn't there an extractor fan somewhere you lot can go and play in?' Knickers was just dizzy.

Having been energetically ushered upstairs by The Wind and returned to The Andrew's room, a clutch of fuzzballs was clamouring around Knickers and Rayon, exhorting them to make it happen all over again.

'Open the doors. Start the motors. Mobilise the mass of The Mum.'

'We want to fly.'

'I'll send you flying,' said Knickers, launching three of the most vocal fuzzballs airborne with a twanged elastic. Rayon was helping Knickers pull off some wool pills she'd become entangled with in all the turmoil. Most of her major threads were all ahoo, making her short-tempered and itchy. The ends of some of Rayon's outer threads were singed after his encounter in the motor with Rusty, but he was mostly still Rayon.

'Looks like Yarn was right,' he said. 'Dust did prevail, and mostly all over you. Hold still.'

'Don't pull so hard,' ordered Knickers. 'Yes, the dense old clump was right. I suppose you just have to trust in entropy and take the long view. Ow! Is this going to take much longer?'

Of Twill, there was no sign. Missing in action. Last seen heroically ushering Silky and her kin into a safe, dark place.

Deposited downstairs in the kitchen, Stour had picked up quite the selection of miscellaneous threads and fabric ends. He was busy entangling himself into a denser, more distinguished and fitting configuration for a dust bunny of his recent experiences. He looked up to see a rough outdoorsy sort of dust bunny landing next to him; strong robust fibres, tightly tangled, too.

'Oh hello,' said Stour. 'Who are you?'

'I just blew in from the garden. I'm Twine.'

'I'm Stour. Are you a piece of string?'

'No, I'm afraid not.'

Everywhere, dust bunnies were settling back into their niches and nooks or, like Twine, finding a warm welcome in a new location. After a lot of wriggling and shoving to get comfortable and secure, a sort of normality returned to the house. As the bright faded, the dark got bigger and crept in past the undrawn curtains, filling the house with one big question – where were the peoples?

A. MICHAEL COLLINS

CHAPTER 18

Apart from the smells, with the baby came the happiest of days. After the tearful, laughing departure of The Vera, the spare room was converted into a nursery, a haven for baby fluff dust bunnies, who brought a delightful, fresh, new pinkness to the old place. The laundry was cranking out fuzzballs every day and any notions of diligent tidying had long been cast aside. In a matter of weeks, everybunny had a smattering of baby talc somewhere about them.

A strangely-scented summer came and went and a winter, too. Then, new dust bunnies started appearing on the scene, entangled from bright, soft baby clothes. After them came romper suit dust bunnies, best-birthday-clothes dust bunnies and now, from time to time, visiting dust bunnies from kindergarten and play dates. New school-wear dust bunnies showed off how smart they looked. A whole new entanglement of dust bunnies was making this place their home.

By virtue of his recent experience, Rayon was now very much more discreet. After his many encounters around the house, he had built up a many-textured cloak of miscellaneous threads around him, some of it good schmutter. He was dark, he was dense, he was dignified. His blue was almost invisible, but he knew it was still there under the fancy new packaging.

Rayon now spent his time in comfortable obscurity, behind a busy multiple power outlet in The Dad's office space. On very dry days, he'd occasionally feel a tingle of static electricity and his adventures would all coming rushing back to him at once. Sometimes, they'd come back so thick and fast they'd blot out the real world and he'd be right there in the tubes again, bright blue and charging.

Stour still visited. Breezing in on The Dad's footwear, maybe after an expedition to the sandpit with The Wee One. Stour was as rugged as could be. He had ballistic nylon threads, he had fibre, he had particles made of rock.

Of Knickers, not much seen but a great deal heard. She'd bulked up to almost three times her size since the baby. She nestled in a corner at the top of the stairs, queen of all she surveyed, dispenser of affectionate guidance to the throng of young dust bunnies that almost smothered her with affection.

'Get back here, you mono-filament,' she would say. 'You're not dense enough to bounce downstairs yet.' Or sometimes, 'You are no more than a recycled beverage bottle, shredded finely. You are a pre-proto dust bunny and not even dusty yet. Get down, sit down, shut up.'

Snap!

'Ow!'

She still had tight elastics for her age. Her electrons, though, still only wandered for Twill. Magnificent Twill, purposeful, decisive Twill. So dense, so well-groomed. Still missing in action.

Twill hadn't come back like the others. He had stayed where he was after he'd rescued Silky. And Satin. And Sheer. And Lacy. At the time of the tidy up, he'd just scooted them all into a niche and squeezed in there with them. After he wriggled in amongst them, however, he knew he would be trapped there forever. He could never bring himself to leave this... this heaven.

He was overwhelmed by the sensuous feel of the dust bunnies' softness, their gentle caresses. He melted at the sublime texture of their soft, pliant threads, their almost liquid smoothness. The richness and lustre of their pearlescent colours bewitched him deeply. Recently, he'd asked and been allowed to borrow a thread or two of Lace, Satin, Sheer or Silk and try them on himself. When inter-twined, he became a dust bunny anew. Transformed from a dust bunny of martial prowess into a dust bunny of beauty. He was gorgeous now.

Many darks and brights later, Yarn, up in the attic, heard the sounds he'd been expecting for a while – the thwump of cardboard boxes being deposited around the house and the long, ripping farts of the packing tape dispenser. Retreating back deeper into his ancient recess, Yarn waited for the coming commotion to blow over, just like all the others.

When the big, burly removal men took the last of the boxes out, they left every room of the house empty of everything. All that remained at Number 42 now were the bare walls, floors and ceilings.

The Andrew, even larger and sprouting hairs on his face, opened the doors, front and back, and gave the floors one final sweep of the broom to get the last of those pesky dust bunnies out.

Most of the last dust bunnies that were swept out the door would catch in twigs or snag terminally on sharp edges. A meagre few would stay airborne for a bright or two, but the first raindrop they encountered would be their last, slapping into the wet ground with the tiniest of splats.

A lucky dust bunny, a very lucky one, might miss the rain. Instead, it would be whisked high into the air by The Wind, perhaps to catch a thermal or an updraught and be lofted skywards above the clouds. Drifting for a number of darks and brights beyond the highest threadcount, a singularly lucky dust bunny might reach the jetstream and circle the globe. Or be taken higher yet, into the stratosphere, it would see our particular ball of dust, before being zapped by the white heat of a falling meteor and adding a few meagre photons of its own to the rushing glory on high.

After the last sweep out, the opportunistic Wind rushed back in,

RAYON THE DUST BUNNY AND A VACUUM ABHORRED

looking to cause disruption one final time. The Wind dashed through doors, sweeping upstairs, darting around each room in turn looking for dust bunnies to disturb, but in vain. It swirled round the kitchen and the lounge, but The Wind moved nothing. Not a particle stirred in its wake.

They're all gone now, not a dust bunny left. All cleaned up. A last, half-hearted gust or two breezes gamely round the downstairs one more time, but fizzles out with nothing. The Wind, all bravado gone, is reduced to a slower, smaller, thinner current of air, wafting meekly out the front door, alone and much diminished.

They are all gone now. Rayon, Knickers, Twill and Stour. All the fuzzballs, each species of entangled thread, every ball, every clump, group, gang, clan or tribe of dust bunnies. Moved out or cleaned up.

The Andrew closes the doors of the house, pushes the keys through the letterbox.

'Bye, bye house.'

The Andrew gets in the car with his mum, dad and little sister and they drive away.

Up in the attic, Yarn notices how quiet the place is now – and no visitors bringing him news from around the house and beyond. 'Never mind,' he sighs to himself, going back to sleep until the commotion starts again. 'Dust will prevail. Dust will prevail.'

Printed in Great Britain
by Amazon